31524

D0541610

Although not origi...
children's author, Geoffrey Trease, born...
has always loved writing and history, and was
able to combine the two in his first children's
novel, *Bows Against the Barons*, published in
1934. Since then he has written over eighty
books for children and a number of adult works,
including novels and a history of London. His
works have appeared in twenty-six countries and
twenty languages. Many were dramatized as
radio serials in the old BBC's *Children's Hour*.

Geoffrey Trease has travelled widely in
Europe, lived in Russia and served in India in the
Second World War. He now lives in Bath, where
his daughter, Jocelyn, is a college lecturer – with
the happy result that he thus maintains constant
touch with his four granddaughters and his
great-grandchildren.

GEOFFREY TREASE

Cloak for  a Spy

MACMILLAN
CHILDREN'S BOOKS

For Miles

First published 1997 by Macmillan Children's Books
a division of Macmillan Publishers Limited
25 Eccleston Place, London SW1W 9NF
and Basingstoke

Associated companies throughout the world

ISBN 0 330 34687 3

3 5 7 9 8 6 4 2

A CIP catalogue record for this book is available from
the British Library.

Typeset by Intype London Ltd
Printed and bound in Great Britain by
Mackays of Chatham plc, Kent

Chapter One

There had been mystery from the first.

Weeks later he recalled the events that led him to the frightening situation in which he then found himself.

He had been racing up the main staircase at home. Suddenly Olivia was above him, arms wide to bar his way, blue eyes big with alarm.

'Giles! You mustn't go into the parlour!'

'Why not?' he asked in a big brother's lordly tone.

'They're having a quarrel! You can hear them.'

He could. Even his mother. This was amazing. His parents never quarrelled. Father laid down the law, Mother meekly agreed. Though sometimes, afterwards, she could be remarkably subtle in getting her own way.

Olivia's hand was on his sleeve. 'It's about *you*.'

1

His heart seemed to turn over. 'Then I'd better go in.'

'Oh, *no* – wait,' she pleaded.

'I must.' He shook himself free. 'Father left word at the stables. Wanted to see me, soon as I came in. You know how he is.'

'Yes,' she said dismayed. 'What have you *done*?'

'I can't think.' At least, he thought he'd done a few of the right things – kicked off his riding boots, washed at the pump in the yard. He must not appear in the parlour smelling of horse-sweat and his own.

Olivia let him go. 'Good luck!' she whispered.

'And don't eavesdrop,' he ordered. 'I'll tell you afterwards – if it's fit for a young girl's ears!' Grim humour, though he felt anything but humorous.

Olivia of course would take no notice. She'd lurk outside, all ears. But his conscience was clear. He paused outside the door. 'It's the *danger* I'm thinking of,' his mother was saying.

'What danger?'

'The many dangers. That a child of mine—'

'Giles is no longer a child . . .'

Dare he interrupt his parents at such a moment? With a silent prayer he turned the doorknob and walked in. The furious dialogue ceased, like a cut ribbon. He pulled off his cap and bowed, first to his mother, then to the towering red-faced man.

'Your pardon, sir. You said to come as soon as—'

'Quite right.' Calm had fallen. His mother had lapsed into the silence she usually kept on such occasions. Giles guessed that she was seething inwardly. 'I have something to tell you,' his father went on. 'You had better sit down.' Giles took a stool. His father resumed his high-backed oak armchair.

'I have been thinking, my boy.' His beard, rust-red against the starched white ruff, jutted with the determination his children knew too well. 'I have reconsidered your request. That I should send you abroad.'

Giles gasped. This sounded too good to be true. Not for his mother, of course. She had been against the idea from the start. She had supported Father with unusual warmth. If he had changed his mind now, no wonder she was upset.

Mother was obsessed with the risks of 'abroad'. If you were not shipwrecked or captured by pirates you'd be robbed or have your throat cut by bandits. Or catch some horrible plague. There were special dangers for Englishmen. Their queen had been proclaimed a heretic. A pope, years ago, had said that her subjects, if loyal to her, were no better than heretics themselves. In a Catholic country where the Inquisition was operating, they could be put on the rack or burnt at the stake. Most likely both.

Father had not based his refusal on Mother's fears.

He was not afraid of 'abroad'. She was exaggerating these risks. Plenty of English gentlemen had travelled widely on the Continent and had returned safely. Father's attitude to foreign parts was one of contempt. Why all this fashionable interest in them? He saw no point in 'abroad' except to provide space for foreigners and keep them out of England. This new fad, that young Englishmen should complete their education with a 'grand tour', traipsing round far-off cities and gawking at ancient buildings, was a waste of money.

What had happened to change his mind? If he had?

'You have learnt all the grammar school can teach you . . .'

Hardly true. But he knew, without undue vanity, that he was one of the brighter boys. He had plenty to learn still, but would have to learn it elsewhere. There was not much more that old

Woodward could teach him. Anyhow, he was almost sixteen now.

'I am not sure about Oxford – or Cambridge. Oxford did not seem of great benefit to your brother.'

Giles was neutral on that. His eyes were on more distant horizons. Father had not been to either university and boasted that he was none the worse for it. Who needed these colleges unless he was becoming a parson?

As to that, Giles was certainly not.

'So – if only to give me more time to decide your future – I think I could do worse than send you off for a few months . . .'

Mother could no longer suppress her feelings. 'He's so *young*,' she wailed.

'You don't imagine I shall let him go *alone*?'

'I shall have a tutor, Mother.' Giles hastened to reassure her. 'Shan't I, Father?'

'Naturally. An experienced, competent person. Used to travelling in foreign parts. Fluent in the language. Indeed, the languages.' Father remembered that not all foreigners spoke the same gibberish. 'You have nothing to fear, my dear. I was discussing the matter a few days ago with Sir Francis Walsingham. He is all in favour of my plan. He thinks I have made an excellent decision. He knows about these things. He was our ambassador in Paris,' said Father impressively.

Mother seemed duly impressed. 'If *he* thinks it is safe . . . But I wish you had told me that before.'

'I have much on my mind just now, my dear.'

'Of course,' she sighed. 'I will say no more.'

Sir Francis was quite the most important person with whom Father could claim any personal friendship. He was close to the Queen. One of her Privy Council. If he approved it must be all right.

Exciting thoughts were racing through Giles's head. 'Where shall I go?' he asked eagerly.

His father blinked; pursed his lips inside that rust-red beard. He had clearly not given much thought to that question. Abroad was abroad. Was any place better than any other? He was clearly playing for time, Giles saw.

'That will be for your tutor to decide.'

'But not Italy!' cried Mother, forgetting her promise to say no more. 'Please God, not *Italy*.'

It was the country where an Englishman was most likely to be tortured or burnt at the stake. It was also the country Giles most wanted to see.

'There are different parts of Italy,' said his father. 'Some are quite safe. They don't all obey every word that comes from Rome. The tutor will take care that the boy is not in danger.'

Giles put the other question uppermost in his mind. 'Who will be my tutor, sir?' He did not fancy having some learned but dreary old schoolmaster leading him across Europe like a performing bear on a chain.

'Sir Francis says he has the very man for us. Mr Martell is coming to see me next week. And you, of course, my dear,' he added tactfully, looking at Mother.

Giles was dismissed. He bowed and left the room, raising his voice to warn Olivia if she were crouching outside. But there was no suspicious scuttling, no hint of flying footsteps in retreat. When the shouting had stopped, and the quieter talk begun, not much would have been heard beyond that massive door.

Chapter Two

He had to find his sister at once, and tell her the great news, but they had no chance to discuss it at length until they took their afternoon walk on the downs.

They went their usual way, southwards to the skyline ridge. It gave them their favourite view – the Channel shimmering away for miles towards France, far away but somehow beckoning.

'I suppose,' he told her, trying to sound casual, 'it's really only to get me out of the way.'

'Out of the *way*?'

'This is rather a full year for Father. He has enough on his plate without having to worry about *my* future.'

It was a pity that fathers had to settle everybody's future. But it seemed to be the law of life.

John's future should have been simple enough. As elder son he would of course inherit the estate. His idleness at Oxford had been only a slight disappointment. 'I am told,' Father had said to reassure Mother, 'that it doesn't matter what you learn there, but what people you meet.'

This year he had arranged for John to go on to Gray's Inn in London and study law. He was not going to be a lawyer, of course, but if you owned land it was best to know a smattering of the subject. He hoped his son would see the sense of that. Law would be more use to him than Latin and Greek. Even so, he had to keep an anxious eye on the lad. In London John seemed to be finding young girls more interesting than old books.

Olivia set problems of quite a different sort.

'There's your marriage to think about,' Giles reminded her.

Olivia made a face. She was still only thirteen, but she knew that he was right.

Parents planned marriages. Young love was for songs and stories, not real life. If you were a king's daughter he tried to marry you off to a foreign prince, so that there would be an alliance between the two countries. You might never see the young man beforehand – indeed, he might even be an *old* man. And you might never see your own family or your own country again afterwards.

For less illustrious folk, like the Taberdars, it was not so bad. But the landed gentry followed much the same principles. Parents arranged things. They wanted connections – like alliances – with similar families, often neighbours but sometimes in a distant county. Olivia's father would have to put up a sizeable dowry, in cash or land, to tempt the parents of the bridegroom. They in turn would settle some land on him, or perhaps he was sure to inherit some later. With luck maybe both. The kinder sort of parents would try, as her mother would, to make sure that the young people knew and liked each other already and were well matched. Others (a father, very often) might declare bluffly that the couple did not know, at their age, what was good for them, but their elders did.

Olivia and Giles knew that her own future was already under discussion, but it was far too early for her to be told of the various possibilities. Though a girl could be married at twelve (for a boy it was fourteen) it would probably be another year before she made her vows at the altar.

Even then she would not at once set up a home with her husband and start a real married life. Though she was already old enough to have a child both families would strongly discourage the idea. Girls who had babies too soon were very apt to lose them. A bride's first duty was to produce a sturdy little boy who would come through the ailments of infancy and provide the estate with an heir.

Olivia knew she must be patient and accept her future when it arrived. For fathers, she felt, children were like playing cards – to be held in the hand and laid on the table when the best moment came. For girls marriage came as a package, the contents uncertain till it was opened, though they might have been long discussed and argued over by the parents on both sides.

She did not resent it when she heard Giles exclaim that he thanked God he was a boy. Few boys were under such great pressures in this matter of marriage. They could, at a pinch, defy their fathers. Nature was on their side. A young woman could not postpone for ever the producing of children. A man could wait until he had made his own way in the world and was free to choose a wife he really loved.

Giles would proably do that. Unless something happened to John, and Giles became heir to the family estate, he had no special responsibilities to anyone. Though Father, she knew, would try to pair Giles off with some local landowner's daughter to mutual advantage.

Today, though, it was more interesting to talk about his projected tour of Europe and what had caused Father's sudden change of mind.

'I think,' she said, 'that he was won over by Sir Francis Walsingham.'

'Really? I know he would take notice of Walsingham's opinion – Walsingham's a very important man . . .'

'Exactly. It wouldn't pay to disagree with him. And he is recommending a tutor for you?'

'Yes. Mr Martell is coming here for Father to inspect him.'

'I'll bet you any money,' said Olivia shrewdly, 'that it will be Mr Martell who is employed.'

'Oh, very likely. If Walsingham thinks so highly of him—'

'So Father will please Walsingham by taking his advice on sending you abroad *and* he'll be providing a post for some man Sir Francis wants to help. Sir Francis should be quite pleased. And Father may be *very* glad to please him.'

'What does that mean, crafty?'

'Can't you see, stupid? Father would love to become *Sir* Anthony Taberdar. What other friend does he have at court?'

Giles had to admit it, she was talking sense. There was a hard little head under that gleaming golden hair.

They were a climbing family, the Taberdars, and he knew his father's ambitious nature. It

12

was obviously time to mount another rung of the ladder.

Until fifty years ago the Taberdars had been prosperous London merchants, in Cheapside. Their chance to move up into the landed gentry had come when the old king fell out with the Pope, who wouldn't give him the divorce he wanted from Katharine of Aragon, to marry Anne Boleyn. As that religious quarrel developed Henry VIII had closed down all the monasteries up and down the country, saying that the monks and nuns had grown slack and were no longer doing any good. It was unfair and untrue in some cases, all too true in others. But the king had his way. He was left with a mass of confiscated wealth, vacant buildings, and thousands of acres of land.

Some of that land went to courtiers and others he wanted to reward. Some went as a gift, the rest was sold, often at bargain prices, because there was such a glut. That was when many families like the Taberdars seized their chance, opened their purses, and made themselves landed gentry.

The garden where Giles and Olivia had played as children was the monks' old herb garden, enlarged and made beautiful. The long straight ponds where they sailed toy boats had once been full of the fish the monks needed for fast days. The prior's house had been converted into a family home. Other buildings were turned into stables and various domestic offices, or pulled down for their stone and leaden roofs.

Local people still called the place 'The Priory', but nowadays it was often referred to just as the 'Taberdars'.

Things had not always been easy in those days, Mother had told the children. There were years of great danger. The family, Giles guessed, must have hung on like grim death, scared lest they be knocked off this high position to which they had climbed.

King Henry died. He was succeeded by his only son, the sickly boy Edward. *He* died when he was no older than Giles was now. His half-sister Mary became queen, a devout Catholic, determined to restore the old religion, with everything just as it had been before. The monks would come back, the Priory would really be a priory again, and soon the Taberdars would be selling cloth in Cheapside once more.

'It must have been *awful*,' said Olivia.

Father, of course, could remember that time. He had been a boy in his teens. In fact his marriage to Mother had been held up for several years – her family had to know how things would go before they could risk a final decision.

Luckily Mary had not lasted. She married a

Spanish prince – the same Philip who was now King of Spain and England's greatest enemy. They had no children, so, when she died after a few years, her half-sister, Elizabeth, became queen. Mary's aim to turn England back to the old religion had not gone far. A number of hapless people had been burnt as heretics, but Mary had had no time to bring monks back to the Priory or anywhere else. The Taberdars could breathe again. It had been a near thing.

Olivia always remembered an afternoon when they played by the fish ponds. Giles had just taught her a nursery rhyme: *Mary, Mary, quite contrary* . . .

The old gardener overheard and stood grinning. 'You'd ha' been for it, my girl, if you'd been caught sayin' that in the old days!'

'Why?'

He explained why the rhyme could have brought trouble, though folks were repeating it in secret all over England.

Mary meant the reigning queen. *Contrary* because she was trying to put everything back, despite what most people wanted.

How does your garden grow? How are things going in this kingdom of yours?

Silver bells and cockle shells . . . The bells sounded at Mass, when the priest held up the bread and wine. The shells were the badges worn by pilgrims to holy places.

And little maids all in a row. The nuns Mary meant to put back in their former convents.

Mother had lived through that period. No wonder she shuddered at the thought of what might happen to Giles in some countries, where people were still being burnt at the stake.

Giles and his sister could sympathize. But such gloomy memories did not lessen his enthusiasm for the adventure. And if only I were a boy, thought Olivia, how gladly would I go with him! But life was not fair, and she supposed she must learn to accept it.

They reached the skyline. The sea spread before them. A galleon was sailing grandly eastwards into the Straits. 'She's one of ours,' said Giles reassuringly. People were always talking about the famous Spanish galleons, but there were English ones too, and Flemish. Further out, making in the same direction, they could see a French caravel.

The west wind set Olivia's skirt flapping. She had hitched it up to climb the hill. It barely brushed the grass, which anyhow was close bitten by the sheep.

A man was silhouetted on the ridge. They walked towards him. He had a horse-drawn sledge, with a barrel of tar and a heap of dead branches and driftwood. He greeted them cheerfully. 'Just renewing the beacon. High time, by the look of it.'

They had never seen it lit. There had been no serious threat of invasion for so many years. Father could just remember the French landing in the Isle of Wight and raiding the Sussex ports, but it had come to nothing.

Olivia asked what would happen if the beacon *were* lit. 'Depends, my dear, whether it was just a general warning or whether the foreigners had actually come ashore.'

'And if they had?'

'I expect you'd load all your valuables into wagons and make for safety. Your dad would arm himself and join the other men. Maybe your brother would go with them.'

'Of course I should!' said Giles.

Seeing Olivia's expression the man said quickly: 'Don't worry, my dear. It won't happen. The French are more likely nowadays to be having a civil war.'

'But the Spaniards? People say—'

'They've got their hands full, fighting the Dutch yonder in the Netherlands. This King Philip threatens a lot but it's only talk. If he tried anything, Drake would see him off.' He stood back to inspect the rebuilt beacon.

'So this is really a waste of time?' said Giles.

'I wouldn't say that, lad.' The man grinned. 'I'm paid for my work. Suits *me*.'

They turned for home. 'I'm glad you won't be going to Spain, anyhow,' said Olivia.

'I don't know about *that*,' said Giles. But he was relieved to think that Spain did not figure in a grand tour.

Chapter Three

'I can't wait to see this Mr Martell,' said Olivia.
'Nor can I,' said Giles. It was five days
before the tutor dismounted in the courtyard,
late on a sunny afternoon.

Giles had prepared himself for someone
elderly and learned. Martell was youngish. He
wore a rapier. His short cloak, doublet and trunk
hose proclaimed a gentleman, though they were
not showy or strikingly fashionable.

There was a second rider, not a servant but
a postboy from some inn. Martell was counting
money into his hand. The man thanked him, and
rode away with both horses.

Olivia appeared now on the front steps with
her parents, framed in the doorway. Giles slipped
across to join them.

Martell swept off his hat and bowed to
Mother. His hair was certainly not grey, but
lightish brown. Tawny, Giles thought, like the
royal lions he had once seen at the Tower.

His parents welcomed the stranger, asking after his journey. 'You rode post, I see,' said Father.

'I thought you'd wish me to come without delay.'

It was, Giles knew, the most expensive way. So many pence per mile for each fresh horse and a little more (threepence per stage, was it?) for the postboy who took it back. But for Father such expense would be nothing.

A servant took Martell's bag, and led him to his room.

The Taberdars went up to the parlour and exchanged first impressions.

'I'd expected someone rather older,' said Mother. Would Martell be in his thirties? Or still only in his twenties?

'It's no matter,' said Father. 'He's a gentleman. He has the speech and manner. Poor, no doubt – or he'd hardly seek service as a tutor. But if Sir Francis recommends him . . .'

Giles guessed that his father would have preferred it if Martell had shown more flourish, perhaps a whiff of high life at court.

'He is not *impressive*,' Father went on. 'A man you could pass in the street and forget you had ever seen him.'

Giles remembered that comment long afterwards and wondered if it was not something Martell deliberately cultivated.

'As to age, that could be a good thing. He looks as though he could handle any little difficulty that might crop up.'

Mother began to exclaim as her forebodings revived. 'No, no,' said Father hastily. 'But anything can happen on the road – even in England. If this man can look after himself, he can look after Giles. I'd sooner send the boy with a young man who wears a rapier than a doddering greybeard who wears spectacles.'

At that moment the gentleman rejoined them, handing Father some letters to read at leisure. Then it was time for supper.

During the meal Mother asked probing questions. 'And are you married, Mr Martell? Have you boys of your own?'

It was a mistake to ask more than one question at a time. It gave Martell the chance to answer one, and conveniently forget the other. Later in the meal Giles noticed this. Martell was a fluent talker. He answered with great courtesy. Whatever he said was interesting, and sometimes amusing. Only afterwards did one realize that he had not always given the precise information that was sought.

It was the second question he pounced on. 'Boys, madam? Alas, no, not yet. I enjoy the company of the young . . .' He made it clear that he would be an ideal companion for a boy touring Europe. 'But, as a Cambridge friend of mine is fond of pointing out, children are hostages to fortune.'

'What an odd remark!'

'My friend is a remarkable person. He came up to Trinity at an unusually young age – thirteen . . .'

'*Thirteen*!' gasped Giles. His brother had gone to university at sixteen.

'Thirteen,' Martell confirmed. 'But he outshone everybody at the sciences – though he thought the teaching wrong—'

'Good heavens!' Father exclaimed with disapproval. 'Who *was* he? What was his name?'

'Bacon, sir.'

The name brought laughter from Giles and Olivia.

'Francis Bacon,' Martell continued. 'Son of Sir Nicholas Bacon, Lord Keeper of the Great Seal . . .'

'Indeed?' The disapproval went out of Father's voice.

'But his uncle, of course, is even better known. Lord Burghley.' Martell dropped the name casually like a pebble into a pool. Burghley was Lord High Treasurer, the Queen's trusted minister. If his tutor had friends like Burghley's nephew he must indeed be (in Father's favourite term) 'well connected'.

Giles ventured into the conversation again. 'You said you were at Cambridge with this gentleman, sir? I thought that Oxford was your university.'

'I attended Cambridge too,' said Martell amiably.

Later, Giles and Olivia wondered if the tutor held one degree or two. Or, as Olivia wickedly suggested, none.

What did that matter? The man seemed to know *everything* – but in the most modest way. He had the real knowledge, that came from life, not musty old books. He had been everywhere. Cities that were only names to them struck off memories of his personal experiences there. Funny or frightening, his stories held them spellbound. In imagination they found themselves walking through those shadowy streets, across those sun-drenched squares. He had obviously been to all these places himself. They almost felt they had been there too.

'It was so real,' said Giles afterwards. The man must have such an observant eye, such a retentive memory.

'Oh, I'm sure everything he told us was true,' Olivia said. 'About Paris, I mean, and the Rhine, the German castles and the Italian palaces – oh, everything. You *are* lucky. You're going to see it all.' She hesitated. 'But when Mother makes him talk about himself, I'm not so sure. I'm sometimes not sure I believe a word of it.'

Women and girls were odd, Giles told himself.

Towards the end of supper Martell suddenly addressed him in fluent French.

For a moment Giles was taken aback. Then he reacted to what was obviously a test of his level of education. After a few stumbling words he managed an adequate response. His parents sat mute, incredulous at his command of the language. Martell turned and smiled at them.

'He has been taught well,' he said. 'And he has been a willing scholar.'

'You think so?' They both looked gratified.

'Indeed yes. And that is important. My friend Bacon says, if you go into a country without some knowledge of its language, you are going to school, not to travel.'

Giles said anxiously, 'But – apart from Latin – French is my *only* foreign language. We'll be going to other countries?'

'Of course.' Martell did not say what other countries. Or what route he planned to follow. 'It will depend,' he said vaguely. 'On the weather. On the news coming from different cities. We are not kings on a royal progress, needing to settle every date and stopping-place months beforehand.' He smiled reassuringly at his hostess. 'If I hear that plague has broken out in a certain region – or a bloody revolution in a city we hoped to see – you would not wish me to take your son there, because it was in some itinerary?'

'Of course not!'

'We rely on your discretion, Mr Martell,' said Father.

'I shall not disappoint you. Or Giles.' He turned back to him. 'We'll be free as the air,' he promised.

The meal finished, they turned to practical details. Giles was allowed to stay. 'After all,' said the tutor. 'He is the person most concerned. Even the preparations are part of his education.' Olivia kept quiet and simply stayed.

Giles would require a passport from the Privy Council, stating the object of his journey. They could be strict about passports, watchful for anyone whose loyalty could be in doubt. Giles, as a youth travelling for his education, should have no problem.

Martell would see to all this, he knew the procedures. He had written out an application. If Mr Taberdar would sign it, he would pass it on to Sir Francis Walsingham. As he was on the Queen's Privy Council, and had himself suggested the tour, there would be no difficulty.

But a passport gave you only permission to 'pass the port' – to leave the country and return. You needed other papers to pass from one foreign state into another. Martell would get these as they moved on. And health certificates – some countries were very particular about them. Martell knew all the procedures.

'What will you do about *money*?' Mother asked. They would need a great deal over several months. Wouldn't it attract robbers? How would they carry such a weight of coinage?

'They won't,' said Father. He was not so far from the family origins as merchants that he did not know how financial arrangements were made. 'When Mr Martell and I have discussed what is needed, it can be done through the foreign money-changers in London. We tell them in which city Mr Martell wants to collect some money. A bill of exchange is made out in triplicate. One copy is kept by him. The other two are posted – separately, in case one is lost – to the person who is to pay out the money. And it might be a good idea,' he said, turning to the tutor, 'if you took one or two letters of credit as well.'

'I can see, sir,' said Martell admiringly, 'that you know your way around!'

'I have never had cause to go around – thank God! – but I know how business is done.'

Giles found all this intensely interesting. It was something he had not been taught at school.

Martell said that the expenses should not be unreasonable. He was not proposing to take servants with them.

The Taberdars looked dubious. 'Is that wise?' asked Mother. His father seemed in two minds. It would be a great economy, but what would people think of two English gentlemen travelling without attendants?

'It's not unusual, sir,' Martell assured him. 'Servants can reduce the value of the whole experience. They are a barrier between the traveller and the people of the country. The boy needs to talk to those people himself, order what he wants, buy in the shops and markets. How else will he learn the language? It can't all be done by reading poetry!'

Giles thought this sounded sensible.

'English servants can be a nuisance,' said Martell. 'They grumble at the foreign food, they scorn the unfamiliar drink. But they get drunk none the less, or ill and cannot be left behind. I believe,' said the tutor firmly, 'in leaving them behind on the first day before going aboard the ship. When I want service I hire it on the spot.'

They would travel light, also. Inn servants would wash their linen, local cobblers would mend their boots and shoes. If new clothes were needed they could buy them on the spot. If Giles was like other youths he had known he would probably enjoy choosing some garment he might never come upon in England.

Olivia exchanged a stealthy smile with her brother. They both thought so too.

'I think now,' said Father, dismissing them, 'Mr Martell and I have some other matters to settle before we sleep.'

After that things moved with what seemed – even to the impatient Giles – almost unbelievable speed. But Mr Martell had personal reasons, it appeared, for beginning the tour as soon as possible. With his experience, and his useful connections at high level, there were no tiresome delays.

Two weeks later they were striding up the gangplank of the little vessel that was to carry them to France. Soon afterwards the sails were spread and the anchor chain rose dripping, link by link. Giles scarcely looked back at the receding cliffs. He was staring ahead, eager for the first glimpse of Normandy.

At his elbow Martell murmured, 'Happy?'

'Oh, *yes*, sir! It's good to be alive!'

But it was his first experience of the sea, and in the next few hours he often wished he was dead.

Chapter Four

In those first days he felt that he was growing up – fast.

It was – oh, everything. The way people spoke to him, looked at him even. Until now his whole life had been spent among people who knew him, and still thought of him as a child, 'the younger son at Taberdars'.

Now he was all the time among strangers, foreigners, who saw him as a young gentleman. The serving men at inns looked at him with different eyes. So did the serving wenches. He found that faintly exciting. But inside he *was* still the recent schoolboy – a grub, he reminded himself, impatient to become a butterfly. He managed to cultivate a slight swagger, suggesting confidence.

'We are not going to gallop across Europe like knights errant,' said Martell. 'When we can join with other travellers and share a coach we shall. We shall save money. We shall have company – and conversation. Good for your French.'

Paris was a hundred and fifty miles away. Creaking and bumping slowly over the roads of Normandy, Giles found that listening to their fellow travellers, straining to catch the meaning and sometimes venturing to join in, was as good a way to pass the time as any. This was French as people of the country spoke it. Words that had never come into lessons at school, words, he suspected, that might have shocked his master if asked to translate them. Occasionally, seeing his baffled expression, Martell would murmur the English equivalent. He was never at a loss.

The effort was worth while. At one wayside inn Giles saw an Englishman trying desperately to make his wants known, using a phrase book printed by Caxton a hundred years before. Giles interpreted for both sides. The Englishman looked vastly impressed.

The inns varied in quality. Martell disliked sharing rooms with strangers but could not always avoid it. At one small hostelry, in a little town overcrowded for a fair, all travellers had to sleep in a common guest-chamber. Surveying the varied company with whom they must pass the night, Martell silently indicated what they had better do. Their money and more valuable possessions should be wrapped in their clean

31

linen and laid in a neat line running down the bed. It would be hard for a thief to remove anything without waking one or other of them.

Usually Martell, being a seasoned traveller, was able to avoid this risk. But only rarely did an inn provide them with a key to their room. Martell carried a pocket door-bolt, an ingenious little device, shaped like a cross, with which he could fasten any door.

On the second morning Giles noticed something he had missed in the candlelight the previous evening. Martell's padded doublet normally concealed a remarkably muscular figure. Before he pulled on his shirt, the light of dawn revealed an old grey scar.

He caught Giles's startled look. 'Ah,' he said smoothly. 'You are wondering? Just an old . . . injury. I acquired it as a boy at football.' He laughed. 'A murderous sport!'

Giles agreed politely. His tutor was normally a mine of information, but sometimes he did not divulge the information you most wanted. 'I *welcome* questions,' he would say warmly if asked something difficult, whether in history, language or literature. There were questions, though, that you did not ask.

An enigmatic character. Giles liked him. He was humorous. But an odd type for a tutor. Was there no way of life he would have preferred?

They reached Paris. 'We shall stay on the Left Bank,' Martell announced. That was on the southern side of the Seine, which flowed through the city, splitting at one point to leave a long thin island where the cathedral of Notre Dame stood.

They found lodging in a quiet side street leading down to the river. Paris was unlike London, where the houses lined the Thames, sometimes overhanging the water. In Paris you could walk along the open quays, where craft of all kinds unloaded their merchandise. You had a clear view across to the royal palace of the Louvre and the rest of the city rising along the other bank.

It was a cheerful, lively area. The crowds seemed largely young and male, students attending the Sorbonne and other colleges of the university.

'They call this the Latin Quarter,' Martell explained, 'because the lectures are given in Latin. The students talk a lot of Latin among themselves – they come from all parts of France, where the language varies a great deal. And many come from other countries.'

'England?' asked Giles.

'A fair number. You might try some of the lectures. See what you think of them.'

'Should I be allowed?'

Martell laughed. 'The lecturers would welcome you. The university pays them no salary – they depend on fees from those who attend their lectures. So the more the merrier!'

'Perhaps I will then.'

Giles was finding it hard to make up his mind about going to a university. One object of his tour was to help him come to a decision. Strolling along the quays with Martell in the sunshine he found Paris attractive.

Several bridges spanned the river. Two narrow islands offered the chance to build them in separate halves. There was the old timber Pont de la Tournelle, upstream, and the Pont St Michel, and, at the downstream end of the Ile de la Cité, the Pont Neuf, very literally the 'new bridge'. It had been started ten years ago but was still unfinished.

'France has been very unsettled – still is,' said Martell. 'There is the constant threat of civil war.' He surveyed the river as they leant on an unfinished stretch of parapet. 'It looks peaceful enough today. But fifteen years ago! We'd have been looking down on *bodies* – hundreds of hacked blood-stained bodies, tossing and turning in the water down there! Women and children, as well as men.'

'St Bartholomew?' Giles whispered.

Mother could never hear Paris mentioned

without recalling that dreadful massacre. It had happened when he himself was still in his cradle. He knew it had been a slaughter of Huguenots, as the French Protestants were called, but he had never been clear about the details.

'Who was actually to blame, sir?'

'The Queen Mother. Catherine de Medici. She's Italian, from Florence.' Martell was staring across at the Louvre. 'She and her favourite son. Henri.'

'The one who's king now?'

Martell nodded. 'Yes. Henri the Third.'

Later, in private, he revealed some interesting facts about the monarch. He liked dressing up in women's clothes. He was frightened of thunder and would hide himself in the cellars. He was not popular, so he kept a faithful body-guard, the Forty-five, and was not above using them to remove his political opponents. He was, to be fair, said Martell sardonically, very fond of small dogs and had quite a collection. He was intelligent enough and a patron of the arts.

But thousands had been butchered in the massacre of St Bartholomew's Day. Giles shuddered. He could understand why his mother felt as she did. Enough terrible things had been done in England in the conflict between Catholics and Protestants, but nothing on this scale.

'I hope there'll be nothing like that while *we're* here.'

Martell reassured him. 'But Philip Sidney *was* caught up in it. And not much older than you.'

'The man who was killed last year in the Netherlands?'

'Yes. He was fighting for the Dutch against the Spaniards. He's a great loss. When the massacre started he hid in Walsingham's house – Walsingham was our ambassador here at the time, that's how I know about it. He was in danger himself. The Queen was in great distress, she thought so much of Sidney. She sent Walsingham a dispatch, to insist on a safe conduct for the boy back to England . . .'

'And did he?'

'Walsingham isn't a man to waste time. He'd already got him out of Paris, with a party bound for Frankfurt. *We* might go there ourselves.'

'Walsingham sounds very good at arranging things.'

'He is.'

Giles wondered if one day he might arrange that knighthood for Father. But he kept the thought to himself.

He adopted Martell's suggestion and went to several lectures by famous scholars. He had to adjust himself to their different pronunciation of Latin. It was hard work and it did not greatly arouse his interest. The charm of Paris had somewhat waned since Martell's talk of the country's outlook. The King had no son. If anything happened to him, the man who had best claim to the crown was the Huguenot leader, Henri of Navarre. But the Catholics would never accept a Protestant, so there was a grim cloud hovering, the chance of civil war.

If Giles decided to attend a foreign university Paris would not be his first choice.

Martell did not cross-examine him on the lectures or even ask a casual question on how he was getting on. For a tutor he seemed very little interested in his pupil's progress. He never went with him to the lectures. He had interests of his own, and seemed content that Giles should be occupied for hours in the lecture halls or talking to other students.

Giles knew that he had been to look up some old friend of Walsingham's, a man named Critory. There were probably other people in Paris he knew from previous visits. And, he told Giles, he had called on the Venetian ambassador to the French court, Giovanna Dolfin, and obtained passports for Venice, should they decide to visit that city.

'It may save time later,' he explained. 'The

Venetians are very strict about these things – one's papers must be in perfect order.'

Giles had been afraid they might not get to Italy. Rome had become dangerous for English Protestants. The present pope was so hot against them. But Martell said that the Venetians were jealous of anyone else's attempts to dictate their policy. Venice would be safe enough.

When, however, he suddenly announced that it was time to be moving on, their destination was to be Germany. Giles would cheer his anxious mother by writing her a letter from Heidelberg. 'Why?' Giles asked.

Martell laughed. 'Because it too has an ancient university – and is famous as a stronghold of the Protestant faith!'

Germany was a patchwork of different states, each with its own princely ruler. Whatever the prince's faith, Catholic or Protestant, was the one the common people were expected to follow.

Heidelberg was on the far side of the Rhine. Giles must get a smattering of German for everyday use. Any lectures would, of course, be in Latin.

Again they travelled mostly by coach, riding only on two days when no vehicle was available. Again the inns varied in quality, though they always got a room to themselves. Giles was adjusting himself to the food, often so different from what he had at home. Even the bread was unfamiliar. He got used to garlic. Instead of the small beer he had in England he began to enjoy wine. When they passed into German territory he was dismayed to find no blankets on the bed. He had to sleep under a second featherbed, it seemed, as well as the one beneath him.

Often the arrangements were really primitive. He asked the porter in his halting German, 'Where is the privy?'

'In the courtyard, sir.'

He walked through and looked round him. There seemed to be no likely doorway. He went back inside. 'Er – where exactly in the courtyard?'

'Anywhere you like, sir,' said the man civilly.

Giles remembered a belt of roadside woodland they had admired as they drew near the village. He decided to stroll back and explore it.

Some nights they stayed in old walled towns with massive gates closed at nightfall. There were formalities for Martell to deal with – passports to show, declarations to be made about their business and destination, and how much money they carried with them. Weapons had to be handed over and receipts accepted. In the morning the weapons had to be collected and a small fee paid. There were heavy penalties if strangers broke the local regulations.

There was a book Martell carried, his constant companion, he said, though Giles had never seen him open it. It had a metal clasp which held it shut. Giles could not read the title for it was in Greek characters, an ancient philosopher's work, Martell explained.

One morning – Giles was alone in the bedroom – idle curiosity led him to pick up the book. He opened the clasp to see what a full page of the elegant Greek type would look like. He turned back the title-page and drew in his breath sharply.

All the other pages had been carefully cut to leave a neat oval hollow. In that nest lay a small wheel-lock pistol, delicate in workmanship, deadly in use.

He was tempted but knew better than to lift it from its nest. It was loaded, the wheel-lock wound up. Hastily he shut the book and put it back where he had seen it, peeping out from under his tutor's pillow.

What an interesting man to have for a tutor! He longed to know more about his background. But an instinct warned him: with Martell it was best to know only as much as he chose to tell you.

Chapter Five

Adventure. That had been his first thought on the day this tour had been dangled before his eyes as a possibility.

There had been some disappointments since. Days of boredom, lip-biting impatience, even resentment against this tutor who so often produced good reasons why they should do or not do this or that.

Now, though, the original excitement was flowing back. They were in Germany, not just a new country, a new world. Not merely a different kingdom, like France or Scotland, with its separate ruler, but a positive patchwork of states, with unfamiliar names that were hard to pronounce and remember – and needed Martell to explain.

Giles knew all about that other patchwork, Italy. He could have sketched a map from memory. The Pope of course reigned in Rome, with a wide spread of papal territories round

him. Venice was a mighty sea-power, the 'Serenissima', the most serene republic. Naples and all
the south, and Sicily, were held by Spain. So was
Milan in the north. Tuscany was an independent
grand duchy, and there was a whole scattering
of little duchies and republics – but an English
gentleman had at least an idea of their names
and where they were.

Not so with Germany, which appeared to
stretch endlessly eastwards, towards Poland and
the mysterious lands of Muscovy. At least they
were not going *that* far.

Giles decided not to worry his head for the
moment about all the German names. Let
Martell explain where necessary. He, himself,
would concentrate on the sights now unrolling
before his eyes.

The Rhine was a revelation. There was no
river to match it at home.

The Thames was fine. He had marvelled at
the swarm of vessels crowding up the last few
miles below the long arched line of London
Bridge, sea-going vessels coming in on the tide
from Holland and Scandinavia and even more
distant countries. The Rhine was wider, and even
more packed with craft, though more of an
inland type.

'The Thames is a gateway,' said Martell, 'and

mighty convenient. But the Rhine is a highway. That's the difference.'

It flowed from the Alpine heights of central Europe to the Low Countries and the sea. It cut across the mountain masses and endless forests of Germany. It linked so many of the principal cities, standing on its banks or on one of its handy tributaries – Strasbourg and Basle, Frankfurt and Cologne and Mainz.

One of the lesser cities was their immediate destination: Heidelberg. They had to cross by ferry to Mannheim, where the Neckar joined the Rhine. Heidelberg was a mere twelve miles up a wooded valley running into the hills.

Giles hoped they might cover this last stretch by some river-craft, but Martell arranged to share a coach with two learned-looking scholars. 'It will be much quicker. The stream is very strong against us.'

Heidelberg stood where the Neckar came plunging out of a mountain gorge and raced down through the flatter country to join the Rhine. A two-hour journey for coach horses would have been slower for a boat fighting against the current.

Giles would not have minded that. He was entranced by the view opening before them. The only hills he knew were the smoothly curving Downs. Here they were mysterious masses of

forest, overhanging like clouds, pierced sometimes with giant spikes of sandstone crag. Often
the sheer hillside turned the pinewoods into the
likeness of a gigantic green tapestry. Sometimes
it was slashed across by narrow slanting belts of
sunshine, where men had made terraces wide
enough to grow vines.

'They grow good grapes here,' said Martell.
'And make good wine.'

They caught glimpses of moving figures.
Often women, to judge from the light voices
pealing clearly across the gulfs of empty air. The
faces were less clear, but there was a consolation,
Giles had to concede, for a seat on the roof of
the coach rather than in a boat half-buried in the
foliage arching over it from the banks.

Left to right, right to left, his eyes roved
freely across this enchanting valley. It seemed a
new world indeed. Would he ever come this way
again? This was the magic of travel – the
newness, the novelty. He wanted to memorize
every detail.

Twenty-five years later, remembering those
moments, he was to laugh aloud.

What would he have said if someone had
confidently assured him that on just such a
golden day in summer – in the very same month
indeed – he would be coming up this identical
stretch of the Neckar valley, scouring the heights

in front for a first glimpse of the turrets of Heidelberg?

He would have been even more disbelieving if he had been told that on this second occasion he would be travelling not in a shabby coach with his tutor and two dry-as-dust professors but in the glittering entourage of an English princess, James the First's vivacious sixteen-year-old daughter, Elizabeth. She would have just married young Frederick the Fifth of Heidelberg, and be bound for her new home there, with this immense party of her countrymen. It would be headed by the Earl and Countess of Arundel, including brilliant people like Inigo Jones, the architect and stage designer, and the lesser-known Giles Taberdar, who had somehow slipped into the party because he knew some German and had been to Heidelberg as a boy.

But on that first morning not even the far-sighted Martell could have foreseen the return visit under such different circumstances.

'The castle,' he said.

In front, closing the eastern end of the town, high above slanting rooftops, the fortress hung like a heraldic shield from the cloudless sky. Its rocky perch must have been several hundred feet above the valley – nothing compared with the wooded heights that flanked it, but enough to dominate town and river squeezed below.

The narrowness of the valley kept road and river in strict parallel. The buildings closed in, the road became a busy street. It was indeed called in German the *Hauptstrasse*, or high street. Little bystreets at frequent intervals ran down to the river.

It seemed a lively place, with shops and taverns and prosperous-looking merchants' houses. They passed a fine church, which Martell thought must be the Peterskirche, built in the days when there was no faith but the old one. It was now the Protestant centre of a mainly Protestant town.

'We must be a little careful,' said Martell. 'There are still churches following the old ways.'

One could believe as one chose. For a generation or two the university had made Heidelberg famous in Europe as a stronghold of Protestant freedom to think and argue as one thought fit.

Giles felt his spirits rising every minute. He was cheered by the animated faces he saw. So many of these people looked so *young*. And they were drawn from so many different places. The fresh complexions and the hair – often blond or coppery – betrayed the lands from which these young men probably came. Holland, Scandinavia, even Scotland ...

They would be meeting at least one Scotsman tonight – one of those 'useful contacts' that in

some mysterious way Martell so often had in places they visited.

Dr John Johnson was apparently a man of some importance in the university.

Perhaps the tutor was beginning to take more interest in the academic aspect of this tour? This visit to a famous seat of learning like Heidelberg would sound well when reported to the family.

Sometimes Martell liked the bustle of a well-run inn. This time, to Giles's disappointment, they were to lodge with one of the town's printers, who was well known as a scholar. Henry Etienne had befriended Philip Sidney some years ago, and was still full of glowing memories of that brilliant youth – as everybody seemed to be who had met him on his travels.

Sad memories now. Sidney had been killed only last year in the Low Countries, leading a charge, sword in hand, against the Spanish troops there.

Martell had known him. 'He married Wal-singham's daughter,' he explained simply. So, thought Giles, that may be why *you* seem to have some of these contacts, and why we are now lodging with this learned printer.

Etienne had talked to them courteously while they enjoyed some light refreshment. But he was clearly needed in the printshop, so, as it was still early to wait upon the Scotsman, they set off to see the castle at the top end of the town.

It was worthy of its superb situation on that airy crag. It had been largely rebuilt by an earlier ruler of Heidelberg, Otto Henry, known as 'Otto the Magnanimous'.

'A great man,' said Martell. He had not stopped short with the graceful new buildings – he had founded a library containing thousands of manuscripts. It was he, largely, who had established the town's reputation. There had been a university for two hundred years, established of course on Catholic lines, but in recent years it had become the great centre for Protestant thinking and the teaching of Calvin.

'It was Calvin who influenced John Knox,' Martell explained, 'and Knox who changed the religious thinking of the Scots . . .'

All this was rather above Giles's head, and he was stifling a yawn, but suddenly things clicked into place and he saw why Scots like Johnson were attracted to Heidelberg. It was Knox who had destroyed the Catholic power in Scotland, driven the Queen of Scots to refuge in England, and set her newborn baby James on the Scottish throne in her place. It was only a few months ago that Mary had been executed – in England – on the charge of plotting with Catholic Spain. It all tied up.

48

On this tour Giles was learning, and learning to understand, a lot more than he had expected.

Chiefly, though, it was his Heidelberg surroundings that fascinated him. They strolled round in the sunshine, looking down on the flashing river and the rooftops of the town.

The castle formed a rough square, with round towers at each angle. There were fine arches and gateways and a courtyard with a beautiful fountain.

Martell pointed out four granite columns. 'They were brought from Charlemagne's palace at Ingelheim.'

That prompted a few words about Charlemagne, on whom Giles was decidedly vague. Martell soon put that right.

'He was the man who saved Christendom from being overrun by barbarians and Saracens,' he said severely. 'The Roman Empire had been overthrown. Charlemagne put it back – with the Pope's blessing – the *Holy* Roman Empire. Which still exists, after nearly eight hundred years! In a sense,' Martell concluded. The tutor did not like to leave loose ends.

He might not have finished then, but Giles strolled on, admiring the beautiful Otto Henry wing which had been that ruler's last contribution before he died. What more would someone add, he wondered, to this superb stronghold? In later years he was to see the place as it was in the brief years of Elizabeth Stuart's brilliant court – the hall, especially, in which English companies were brought over to perform plays by Shakespeare.

The end of this busy day was a supper with the Scotsman.

How good it was to meet someone fresh with whom they could talk their own language – even if Johnson's broad Scots was a shade puzzling at times.

The students were grouped into three 'nations', rather like the colleges at Oxford and Cambridge, but not, it seemed, with the same elaborate disciplines. The Heidelberg students were drawn here with a keener purpose. Giles rather liked the sound of it.

'We are specially known for our teaching of law,' said Johnson.

'Indeed you are,' said Martell. 'But,' he added, 'it is Roman law. And that would be useless to Giles.' He seemed suddenly to have cooled off towards Heidelberg now that Giles was warming to the place.

Roman law, the tutor admitted, was still the basis in most countries, though it must now be a thousand years since the emperor Justinian had gathered a team of experts and laid it down clearly. Almost every legal system still followed it, including Scotland. But the English in their contrary way had preferred to build up their own law, by custom and by act of Parliament. If Giles wanted to study law he had better follow his elder brother to one of the Inns of Court in London. He would be wasting his time at Heidelberg.

And yours too, Giles said to himself. Martell liked to move on.

'I should like to attend some of the lectures,' said Giles wickedly.

'Of course, why not?' said Martell. 'It is your education that must come first at all times!'

'Of course.' Giles kept his voice bland.

A little later, though, a casual question gave the tutor a chance to get back to the Holy Roman Empire and tie up a loose end or two.

Giles had asked Dr Johnson why the enlightened ruler of this city was always referred to as the 'Elector'.

'The Elector Palatine,' said the Scot. 'The Palatinate is the name for all this area.'

'And he is one of the seven German rulers,' put in Martell swiftly, 'who can vote when a new emperor has to be chosen.'

Vote? Giles sat up. This was something interesting. *Vote* – for an emperor?

The imperial power then did not pass from father to son like a crown. Seven great cities had long ago been given the right to choose the next emperor when a vacancy occurred.

'It was vital,' said Johnson. Some states were Catholic, some were Protestant. Neither the Pope nor anyone else must get permanent power over the Empire.

Yes, this *was* interesting. It explained things Giles had never understood.

Years before he was born, one of these emperors, the mighty Charles the Fifth, had actually resigned his office because he had too *much* power, and being a solemn conscientious man could no longer bear the responsibility. How could a small boy understand such a thing? Now, as his tutor and the Scotsman talked over these old matters, Giles saw.

Charles had been king of Spain anyhow. He held half Italy, he claimed the Netherlands, great tracts of Germany, the whole new world that the Spaniards had discovered and conquered beyond the Atlantic. He had even stormed the pirate stronghold of Tunis and tried to extend his sway in North Africa. No wonder that in the end it had all become too much.

Ancient history? Hardly, Giles realized, as the two men talked on.

In the last few months he had passed from his own childhood to the adult world. He was eager to understand, so that he could hold his own when these matters were discussed. For they still affected the world around him, in which he had to live.

The emperor's son had been Philip – that Philip of Spain who was still so very much alive, a figure of dread in some quarters, the arch-enemy of England.

If the empire passed from father to son Philip would be emperor today. Luckily it did not. When Charles abdicated he tried hard to get his son the vacancy. But the Electors would not have him. Several, like the one at Heidelberg, were staunch Protestants – and Philip, they reckoned, was too fanatical in his Catholic faith.

Giles was particularly interested in the heat with which Martell spoke out against the Spanish king. Normally the tutor was so cool. Sometimes, indeed, Giles wondered if he was voicing his true opinion or deliberately taking another line so that all points of view got fair consideration. It was his educational method.

But Philip – presumably because of his hostility to England – stirred Martell to a feeling he could not hide.

Philip had even come over to England and married Queen Mary because she too was a devout Catholic, struggling to undo the Protestant changes started under Edward the Sixth.

If Mary had lived – or at least borne Philip a child – the change might have been achieved.

'And when Mary died he would have been willing to marry Elizabeth,' said Martell, 'provided she would change *her* faith!'

That desperate scheme had come to nothing. Philip still dreamed of somehow getting England back into the Catholic fold, though Elizabeth had been declared a heretic.

Johnson was nodding gravely while the tutor held forth. Philip, of course, was just as much the enemy of Scotland, that even greater hotbed of Protestant heresy. 'But England has Francis Drake,' chuckled Martell, with a return to his normal cool manner.

Altogether Giles found it an instructive evening. He had learnt a lot about the complex political set-up of central Europe – and possibly about this companion who sometimes puzzled him.

Chapter Six

The charm of Heidelberg never weakened.

With a mere tilt of the head his fancy could soar into that upper realm of sandstone crag and feathery conifer. And here below, in the streets and little squares, there was the constant bustle of the townsfolk and the hubbub of the students, matching the noisy rush of the Neckar swirling past the end of every byway.

It was good, when he started to attend some lectures, to be among so many *young* people again. In fact many must have been several years older than himself. They had reached Heidelberg after drifting across Europe and trying other universities. The point was that they were unattached and free, far from their homes and not yet pegged into any regular way of life.

None spoke English, many had scarcely heard of England. They communicated in Latin, with occasional scraps of German picked up in their wanderings. They spoke their minds freely, often passionately. Who was to stop them?

After that first day Giles saw little of Martell. Once his charge was launched into the daily round of the university the tutor seemed to feel no more responsibility for his education. So there were no more lengthy explanations of the Empire. Giles had seldom been bored – he was keen enough to learn and Martell's dry humour made things more interesting – but the younger company made a change. Probably his companion had other friends beside Johnson among the senior men – or would find them. He was a man who would.

Only one thing was lacking in this world of youth: one saw no girls except those who brought round the mugs of beer and the savoury snacks.

'*Girls?*' cried a young Dane. 'How could there be girls? In a university? *Studying?*'

Just to be awkward Giles challenged this. Why not? Girls – given the chance – could study as well as men. His own queen, Elizabeth of England, had been learning Latin, French too, and Italian, before she was ten. Then Greek, though even its alphabet was different. Later, he had heard, she had turned to Spanish. She knew some German – she spoke it badly, but people did not point that out. (He had heard this from

Martell.) The queen was proud of her foreign languages, but many other high-born ladies were fluent too.

'Oh, languages,' admitted Henrik. 'Great ladies need them, I expect. But what do they want with philosophy and theology?'

Universities existed to train priests or religious teachers. What use would the training be to a female?

The youth was so obviously right, Giles knew that he himself was arguing only for the sake of argument. But that could be amusing too.

Martell laughed when he was told of this conversation. 'Henrik was so narrow-minded,' said Giles. 'Asked how I could possibly be interested in *women*!' He spoke the last word in the tone of utter contempt the Dane had used.

'And what did you answer?'

'The best way to floor anyone like that is to bring out some weighty quotation from a famous ancient author that he daren't contradict.'

'So . . .'

'I remembered what Terence wrote in his comedy: *Homo sum: humani nil a me alienum puto*.'

Martell's laugh was almost a roar as he translated the Latin: ' "I am a man. I reckon everything human is my concern." And he accepted that?'

Giles grinned. 'Yes. Even the *homo sum*! He could hardly argue about that. He's only a year or two older than me.'

And yet, somehow, Giles admitted to himself, these foreign students *did* often seem much older. They were so serious. They would wrangle for hours after sitting through one of those endless lectures on religious doctrine, hurling long words at each other like 'predestination'. Was it settled when you were born that you were one of God's 'elect' and sure of your eventual place in Heaven? Or did you have to earn that place by your 'works' throughout your earthly life?

Only once did he allow himself to grumble to his tutor.

'They only seem interested in the *next* world,' he burst out. 'I thought I was coming on this tour to see *this* world and learn all about it!'

'Your preference is evident,' said Martell dryly. 'I am inclined to share it.'

Yes, thought Giles. The man often puzzled him, could sometimes be maddening, but at bottom Martell was all right.

He seemed particularly so on the day he handed Giles a letter from home. It had come with a batch of mail for himself. From – Giles was pretty certain – his influential friend Walsingham.

It made a vast difference having a contact like that. People of course were constantly sending each other letters to and fro across Europe. Merchants who had business mail crisscrossing all the time. Scholars in Oxford and Cambridge and all these innumerable foreign seats of learning. And obviously governments, ambassadors and suchlike.

For ordinary people it was possible but more difficult. 'Especially,' said the tutor, 'if you are like us, constantly on the move from place to place.' It took a little arranging.

He did not like committing himself. Giles had noticed that. Departures could be at short notice, destinations suddenly altered. 'Ideally,' said Martell, 'we should be free as the air.'

Giles agreed. It made it difficult, of course, to maintain contact with home but, much as he loved everybody, this was the least of his concerns. He assumed all was well with them, he knew he was all right himself, and it might have been very tedious to be tied down to a rigid programme of dates and destinations. Martell's fortunate friendship with an important person like Sir Francis Walsingham helped to lessen their isolation. In any real emergency the tutor could probably make use of the messenger network linking the Privy Council secretary with his representatives in foreign capitals.

The long letter from home was welcome, but not sensational. Everyone was in good health. He was much missed. They hoped etcetera etcetera. Only in the postscript which his father had allowed Olivia to add was there a real hint of wistful warmth and affection. There was a lot to be said for girls. Martell said his reply must be ready tomorrow. He answered Olivia's postscript with an attempt to convey some of his feelings about the tour, especially Heidelberg.

There were times, to tell the truth, when these students became a little wearisome. They were often so earnest, so argumentative. In the lectures they scribbled frenziedly, determined to miss no word that fell from the lips of the learned men addressing them. Yet they showed little respect for the professors, whatever their international fame. If they spoke too quickly the students would start rapping on their desks in a protest which grew to a riotous crescendo.

Giles's sympathies were divided. Some lecturers – ill-paid if their audiences were small – did gabble to get the task over. If he had wanted to note every word of their eloquent Latin he might have been glad to slow them down. But usually he was as thankful to get to the end as the lecturer obviously was. The disrespectful rapping on the desks shocked him. He could not imagine that it happened at Oxford.

Friendship with his fellow students did not develop as he had hoped. They had little interest in telling him about their own countries, still less in hearing about his own. A casual friendly drink led quickly into a keen debate on philosophy or Protestant doctrine. A walk in the forest developed in the same way. The crags, the soaring pines, the soft murmur of the water far below, made no impression upon his companions.

Martell never offered to walk with him. Perhaps he did not wish to intrude on Giles's attempts to mix with these young men. More likely, Giles guessed, he preferred the society of the Scotsman and the other senior members of the university. Martell was a good listener. He liked to merge into the background that appealed to him. Some days Giles hardly saw him.

So he settled for his own company, perhaps with a book. At least there were plenty of books in the printer's house, though few as light – in either sense – as he could have wished. One afternoon, though, he found flesh-and-blood companionship of a kind he had not dared to hope for.

He had crossed the river and climbed the

Philosophers' Way. It was a steep path, winding up through the forest to the old monastery of St Michael on a summit with especially fine views up and down the valley.

Halfway up he saw the two girls. They were sprawled on the grass beside the track, their baskets glistening with wild berries they had been gathering. They barely raised their heads – one dark, one flaxen – at his approach. They seemed very intent on something. When the path brought him so close that he could glance down at them he saw that the dark girl was extracting a thorn from her companion's foot.

They did not acknowledge his existence and he thought – reluctantly – that it might be unwise to acknowledge theirs. From the start of their journey, Martell had warned him against getting mixed up in any way with the female inhabitants of any foreign land through which they might travel. One ordered food and drink, one held out a shirt to be washed or something else to be darned, one indicated any other simple requirement. But it was better to leave it at that, even in a country like France where one knew the language.

'Nations differ in their manners,' said Martell. 'What would be harmless in England – a joke, an innocent passing of the time of day – can be taken amiss by some of these foreigners.

Especially by their menfolk. You do not want to end up with a knife between your shoulder blades?'

Giles did not.

So, with some reluctance (after all, these laughing lasses had no menfolk with them), he trudged stolidly past them, gaze firmly fixed on the monastery showing through the trees above. 'Fix your mind on higher things,' he told himself.

He had gone only a few yards further when a loud scream stopped him in his tracks. He turned – what boy would not have done?

The girls were on their feet. The flaxen-haired one on her bare foot, the dark one restraining her with outstretched arms, both heads bent to peer down into the leafy gulf below them.

'*Nein, Frieda! Nein!*' pleaded the dark girl. Yet mingled with the panic in her voice was there a hint of laughter? It did not occur to Giles till afterwards. At that moment the drama was too compelling. He turned and ran back, pulling up in the nick of time when he saw the full extent of the drop.

The fair girl's slipper itself had not fallen far. It had lodged in the branches of a bush just below. It could be reached by anyone with a sure footing and a cool head for heights.

That was evidently what its owner thought.

The dark friend evidently disagreed. She suddenly became aware of Giles at her elbow and poured out a stream of hysterical German.

'Leave it to me,' he said tersely. If she did not know even that much English she understood his meaning. She subsided into anxious twitterings, in which the fair girl joined.

They both stood and watched. It took him only a few moments to size up the situation, lower himself carefully with the right handholds, climb back with the slipper, and return it to its owner with a courtly bow.

Either that bow, or the sheer release of tension, caused both girls to dissolve into uncontrollable laughter. They collapsed on the grass again, patting a space between them. He could hardly stand over them, staring down, so he accepted the invitation – and the berries with which they rewarded him from their baskets.

He looked from one to the other. 'And whose idea was it to throw down that slipper?' he demanded. But he put the question in Latin, guessing that neither of them would understand. They did not, but it relieved his feelings to show, if only to himself, that he had seen through the trick. The slipper had not been sent flying by some accidental kick. It had been dropped carefully into that bush with an eye to easy recovery.

By the dark girl, Lise, he felt sure. Frieda's

confusion was half genuine. Her friend's trick had taken her by surprise, but she had quickly fallen in with it. And it had worked. The contact had been made. No one had to seem shameless.

A pity the girls did *not* know Latin. Though the vocabulary of the lecture room would not have been much use here. But in his short time in Heidelberg he had picked up a smattering of everyday German. He could answer some of their questions. They had never met an English boy and were fascinated. What with sign language and smiles, explosions of mirth at obvious misunderstandings, a lively conversation developed. It was ended only when the chiming of a clock in the city below brought the girls scrambling to their feet.

Giles felt no desire to resume his climb to the monastery of St Michael. He turned downhill with Frieda and Lise. The laughter and chatter continued until the first outlying houses became visible through the trees. At a bend in the path the girls paused, as if by unspoken agreement, faced him and dropped a little curtsey. But their eyes were still dancing and contained no hint of final farewell.

Anyhow, thought Giles, I shall walk this way tomorrow at the same hour, and we'll just see.

The girls tripped away. He waited some minutes until their footsteps and laughter had faded round the bend. Then he continued on his way down into Heidelberg. Yes, a good place, he thought contentedly.

But it was to be twenty-five years before he walked beside that river again.

'So *here* you are,' said Martell when they met at supper. 'A change of plan! We are leaving in the morning – for Frankfurt.'

Chapter Seven

For some moments Giles was – fortunately – speechless.

This maddening Martell! Without any discussion, he had announced a change of plan which Giles must accept with the unquestioning meekness of a child.

The printer was speaking now. It was impossible to interrupt. Giles had time to think. His mind was racing – and towards a calmer response.

He had just met those girls. But he had no certainty of meeting them again. Even if he did, would anything interesting come of it? One thing at least was sure – Martell had not seen them, and, however much he might have disapproved of the association, he could hardly have arranged this sudden departure to Frankfurt to scotch it.

Giles soon realized that tomorrow's plan was no crafty scheme of Martell's but a well-meant effort in his pupil's interests.

67

'Master Etienne has business in Frankfurt,' he explained.

'All printers have business in Frankfurt,' said their host. 'Always! It is a great city, my boy, one you should see. So I suggested you should both travel with me in the morning.'

'You were complaining,' said the tutor with a chuckle, 'that the Heidelberg students were interested only in the next world. In Frankfurt it is quite different. It will be good for you to have a change.'

Frankfurt was very much more concerned with the world around them. A trading city, with tentacles reaching out all over Christendom – and far beyond.

'You will meet people, and pick up news, from everywhere,' said the printer enthusiastically. 'The book fairs bring people from every city. I dare not miss them! Printers and booksellers – not only from every part of Germany but from Italy and France and the Low Countries, England even.' He chuckled. 'And what a place for gossip! We are constantly reminded, are we not, Matthew, that not all useful knowledge comes out of books?'

'We are indeed.'

Frankfurt was a mere fifty or sixty miles to the north. The city lay on another of the Rhine's eastern tributaries, but the Main flowed through country very different from the craggy gorge at Heidelberg. There were rich orchard lands as well as forest. The high hills were more of a brooding presence on far-off horizons.

The city was vastly bigger than Heidelberg, the river wider with a bridge of fourteen arches. The printer pointed out ancient fortifications and a stretch of the moat. Frankfurt had been made a free city of the Empire over two hundred years ago.

'It's here that a new emperor is elected,' said Martell. He pointed out the cathedral with its magnificent tower. 'That's where the ceremony takes place.'

So it was in there, years ago, that the Electors had shown their independence and voted against Philip of Spain succeeding his father as emperor and continuing the Spanish domination of Europe.

Frankfurt was about power, a city of that real world which he was finding of much greater interest than the world to come which kept them arguing so endlessly at Heidelberg.

They passed the Romerberg, the great square on a mound in the middle of the city where the book fairs and similar gatherings were held. It was dominated by the Romer, the *Rathaus*, or town hall, its gables rising in steps. All round stood imposing houses, homes of the wealthier merchants.

Their Heidelberg host was to stay in one of these, as guest of a prominent Frankfurt bookseller. But, as he explained, there would be no room for Martell and his pupil. The house would be packed with leading people in the trade. Martell accepted these apologies gracefully – one might almost say 'gratefully', Giles thought. Martell had not brought him to Frankfurt to listen to incessant book-talk. And Martell liked freedom to be left to his own devices.

They found a room to themselves at a little inn called the Three Stars. It was not far from the Romerberg, and Giles himself spent some pleasant hours wandering down the endless rows of stalls ranged neatly across the mound. He had seen, in London, the array of bookstalls in St Paul's Churchyard, but nothing to rival this three-week concentration. Venice alone seemed to have sent a host of competing printers and dealers. He was particularly taken with the handy little pocket-sized Greek classics – tragedies and comedies, history and philosophy, poetry ranging from two-line epigrams to the long rolling epics like Homer's *Iliad*, all set in that graceful Greek type of which he could not decipher a syllable.

All those alphas and betas and omegas!

Wrapped up in them, tantalizingly, were the original books and plays, written so many centuries ago, when even the ingenious Greeks had never thought of the printing press. He sighed. He would have liked to learn Greek – but there was so much to learn, and do, in life. He knew in his heart that he would never be a single-minded scholar.

'Frankfurt must be *dead*,' he said to Martell, 'when the book fair packs up and goes.'

His tutor laughed. 'There are other sorts of fair. And the trade that just goes on, day after day.'

Trade meant money, money meant power – that was why Frankfurt, without great armies or fleets, was so important. He told Giles of one man, Johann von Bodeck, who had become prominent in the city. He came of a noble Prussian family but his aptitude for business had won him far more power than his relatives.

'He buys – and resells,' Martell explained. 'He buys mercury from Nuremberg and sells it in Amsterdam, he ships rye from Amsterdam to Genoa and sells wool to Amsterdam which he has bought in Spain. The stuff may never pass through Frankfurt,' he grinned as Giles goggled. 'He can do it all with a stroke of the pen. Wherever you are, whatever it is – silk or cinnamon,

71

iron or indigo – if you can pay, von Bodeck can supply.'

Money on that scale meant power.

'Our own queen could do with it,' said Martell sadly.

'The Queen?'

'She has no money – not on the Frankfurt scale. She cannot afford to keep up a fleet of her own. If she needs warships she has to commission them. While the danger lasts. She must scrimp and scrape, our beloved Gloriana. Whereas Philip of Spain . . .' He paused and shrugged. 'Yes, money is power.'

You could learn things in Frankfurt, Giles realized, that were not taught in the lectures at Heidelberg.

Would they be going back there, he wondered? As usual, Martell was vague. He would discuss possible destinations and their advantages but he did not invite opinions or preferences. Giles accepted that. It was the way of life. Teachers decided, pupils obeyed.

This time, however, Martell was to have decision forced upon him.

They were taking a late-evening stroll together through the streets. Martell pulled up suddenly, gripping his pupil's arm.

'A man I know . . .'

Giles saw a figure vanishing into a tavern called the Griffin.

'This is lucky,' said Martell rapidly. 'I had hoped to see him in Strasburg.'

So we're going to Strasburg, thought Giles. Or *are* we, he asked himself cynically? Perhaps I shan't see Strasburg now, if he's seen the friend he wanted to tonight?

'Can you amuse yourself for an hour?' Martell was unusually considerate. 'Dr Lobetius is a dry old stick – but he and I will have things to talk about.'

'Of course, sir! In about an hour, then?'

'I may be glad to be rescued by then!'

Giles took a leisurely turn round the city, the streets getting livelier as the dusk gathered. The looming buildings were jewelled with lighted windows, outdoor lanterns and flaring torches. He stood on the long arched bridge, looking at the reflections gleaming in the Main. With so many foreign strangers at the fair it was interesting to eavesdrop on their comments.

He was back at the Griffin as the church clocks struck the hour. The tavern was crowded now. It was all he could do to edge through the doorway and peer from its shadows into the bright interior.

Two men blocked his way, an aproned serving man listening to an elegant gentleman,

73

who Giles guessed might well be a Spaniard. He wore his hair rather longer over his ears than most men and the brim of his hat had narrowed almost to vanishing point. He was talking German to the serving man, but with what could well have been a Spanish accent. Latin, as Giles had found, was only really useful with men of education.

His own German was still scanty and he could make out only scraps of their dialogue, but the sudden mention of the name Lobetius alerted him.

'And the man with him – English, you thought?'

The serving man did not know. He was not lodged at the Griffin. Giles caught a reference to the Three Stars. He restrained the natural impulse to push forward and be helpful. With Martell it might be wiser not to.

'He is much taken with our local drink – the apple wine,' said the serving man chattily. Giles gathered that one of the glasses on his tray was on its way to the Englishman. 'If your Excellency will excuse me . . .' He turned away to fill some tankards with beer.

'Of course,' said the Spaniard. But he stayed where he was.

Giles thought it might be best to back silently into the darkness outside. Give Martell time to drink his second glass of apple wine. The serving man was busily loading his tray with a variety of other orders. A coin glinted briefly in the Spaniard's hand. The German muttered his thanks. Giles slipped out of the doorway just as the Spaniard turned. He strode past Giles without a glance.

Odd, he was pulling on his glove again – yet the other hand was bare. Why wear only one glove? Or any glove on such a close evening? A most trivial question, which only came back to him later. His concern now was to present himself at Martell's table and give his tutor an excuse, if he wanted one, to end his conversation with this Lobetius.

That went smoothly enough. The two men were chatting cordially, but Giles was developing a sixth sense nowadays which told him when Martell felt that a topic was exhausted and he would like to move on. Giles was duly presented to the scholarly stranger, asked a few questions, and complimented on his Latin. Then the farewells were spoken and the English pair set out for their own lodging.

'A long day,' said Martell with a yawn. 'But not without profit. Especially this past hour.'

'Dr Lobetius?'

'It was most fortunate. Most informative.' The tutor yawned again. He stumbled on the threshold of the Three Stars. His speech was a little slurred. Had Martell been a stranger, Giles would not have wondered. But in all their travels so far he had never seen his tutor the worse for drink. The man could hold his own in the most hard-drinking company, but, as he had confided to his pupil, there was a knack of *seeming* to drink much more than one did, and not appear a spoilsport.

Two or three glasses of apple wine could scarcely have produced this effect. Martell was dragging himself up the staircase as though his legs had turned to lead. He almost collapsed on his bed. He got out an incoherent remark about 'm' boots', fell back on the pillow and was gone.

For the next two or three minutes Giles was in a panic. Surely Martell *could* not be drunk, though he showed all the signs?

Obediently Giles pulled his boots off. He made fast the door with that ingenious cross-shaped bolt of Martell's. No one must come in and see him in this condition. But who *would* come in before tomorrow, when surely his tutor would have slept it off?

Who indeed? Suddenly the light dawned. The events of the last hour or two reshuffled themselves in his memory and offered a new picture that made sense.

The Spaniard who had been interested in

the unknown Englishman sitting with Lobetius! Could he possibly? Giles remembered the shadowy entrance of the Griffin, the serving man collecting his assortment of drinks . . . the apple wine ordered by Martell . . .

Suppose someone was planning to come to this room tonight? Not – most certainly – to talk to Martell, but more likely to go through his belongings while he slept? Thinking back to the ill-lit entrance hall Giles realized how easily the Spaniard could have slipped something, a powder perhaps, into Martell's glass. He would have discovered later that the Englishman had not a room to himself, but he had not struck Giles as the sort who would let a boy wreck his plan. If he did not find Giles deep in the natural sleep of youth he would make sure he did not interfere.

As Giles's imagination developed this theory it seemed less and less likely that he would get any sleep, natural or otherwise.

He must not. Simply must not. He could think of no one to turn to. Who would have believed such an unlikely story? The next few hours would show if there was any truth in it. He must hold that door against any intruder. By morning, pray God, Martell would be himself again. There was no sign that he had been poisoned or had become ill in any way. His breathing was deep but regular.

Giles surveyed the room by the light of its single candle.

He unclasped the hollowed-out Greek book and this time very gingerly removed the little pistol concealed inside. Was it loaded? At least, if anyone got into the room, the mere sight of it might deter him. Much better, though, if nobody did.

He checked the door-bolt. It was firm. Silently he dragged over an oak chest as a barricade. He was not sure what any intruder would be looking for. Money? Private papers? Martell had a leather case into which he sometimes delved for letters and documents, official permits and suchlike. Giles could do no more than thrust it under the bed.

Midnight struck. Giles put out the candle and sat down on the truckle bed under the window. Was he being fanciful? If nothing happened would he say anything to Martell? There had been something mysterious about the Spaniard. He had obviously known Lobetius – but had made no move to go and greet him. He had clearly been interested in Martell's identity. Martell never seemed to like that. And Martell would surely admit that there had been something peculiar about his sudden rush of sleepiness?

One o'clock struck. And soon afterwards – *was* it fancy? – he heard the faintest, most furtive, movement on the stairs.

Heart in mouth, he crept across the dark room to the door. He listened intently. He laid his palm on the woodwork, felt the tiny strain and tremor of someone's pressure outside.

The door-bolt held. Now he heard whispers. That was bad. So there were two men outside. One murmured softly, '*Ventana*?' The Frankfurt book fair was a positive tower of Babel and Giles had picked up many an odd word. *Ventana* was Spanish for window.

He went cold. He had not studied the window or what chance it would offer to a determined intruder. It suggested alarming possibilities.

He stole across to his bed, leant across, and stuck his head out into the night. Yes, he could see well enough in the starlight. A man could creep along the parapet outside. He closed the casement and made it fast – but how long would it keep out a man determined to get in?

Despairingly he returned to the big bed and bent over his tutor, praying silently for some sign that he was returning to consciousness. The steady breathing offered no hope.

Suddenly he thought, angry at his own stupidity: 'Why am I creeping about like this? Pretending that *I'm* asleep too? If they knew I was awake...' A further idea struck him. 'If they thought *he* was awake...'

He had heard the men outside whispering. What if they heard *him* whispering? A pity Martell could not whisper too! If they thought there were two people in the room awake, and waiting for them, ready, armed...

It could be done. Anyhow, it could be tried.

At school, acting in plays, he had often played old men, kings and so on, deepening his voice. 'Better make fast that window,' he said aloud. 'I will, sir,' he answered in his normal tone. He went back to the window, reopened it, and slammed it shut.

All sound from the staircase had stopped abruptly. The strangers could be in no doubt that someone was wide awake in the room – two, if his trick had succeeded.

'Here are your pistols, sir,' he added, hoping that one of the strangers might understand that much English. For a minute or two he kept up the make-believe dialogue, though he soon felt certain that there was no audience outside the barricaded door. He sat down on his bed then, trembling in every limb. But no menacing faces appeared at the window either.

Afterwards he remembered nothing more until he woke in the dawn light, with Martell shouting heartily and incredulously: 'Not you as well? What on earth got into us both?'

Chapter Eight

Giles explained in an injured tone that in his own case this log-like stupor could have lasted only a few hours. He remembered hearing a clock strike three. Then, feeling sure that the strangers had given up, he had sunk into exhausted sleep.

If Martell had not already been wide awake, what Giles said would certainly have roused him.

'These men,' he exclaimed. 'But no, you could not see them. The man at the Griffin! At least you can describe *him*.'

Giles did his best. 'Mostly he had his back to me. But he was thinnish, middle-aged, a gentleman, a Spaniard, I reckoned. One unusual thing – he was wearing only one glove.'

The effect of this remark was startling.

Martell's eyes were riveted upon him. In a changed tone he said: 'On which hand?'

Giles had to think back. 'Oh, the right.'

'Then it *would* be Gonzalo!'

His tone made Giles stare. 'Do you know him, sir?'

'I know *of* him. Our paths have never crossed. He's famous for his single glove.' He took pity on Giles's curiosity. 'You have heard of Lepanto? Though you were scarcely born then.'

'It was a great naval battle, wasn't it? Off the coast of Greece. The fleets of Venice and Genoa, with lots of Spaniards helping them – they defeated the Turks, didn't they?'

'They certainly did. But Don Gonzalo had his right hand nearly sliced off by a Turk's scimitar—'

'This man had his,' said Giles disappointed. 'He held out a coin to the servant.'

'A good surgeon saved his hand. But not the use of his thumb. Gonzalo had been one of the best swordsmen in Spain. It spelt the end of that. Imagine! And he was – is – a vain man.'

'Surely it didn't finish his career as a soldier? He could still lead troops as an officer – even become a great commander?'

'Of course. And in a sense he has. But in a different field. He works for the Spanish viceroy in Milan. He is head of his counter-espionage organization. He has a little army of spies and counter-spies.'

Giles listened with racing mind. Martell sat

on his bed opposite, studying his expression. He went on:

'I think I owe you an apology, lad. What you did for me last night was splendid. There's too much play-acting in my life. I can't keep it up any longer with you. You must have been forming your own suspicions about me?'

Giles made a careful answer. 'I mean no disrespect, sir – I've learnt a lot from you, I'm sure you are a fine scholar – but I don't believe you're much concerned with my education. I think this whole tour is really a cover for something else – I'm being used as a cover . . .'

Martell nodded. 'And you resent that? Naturally.'

'If you are spying for England, sir, I'd rather be trusted as a companion – not used as a cloak!'

'I'm sure you would!' Martell looked pleased but troubled. 'What a problem you set me! One I must settle – instantly.'

He must leave Frankfurt at once, covering his tracks. Gonzalo, though foiled last night, would be hot on his trail. By now he would have discovered Martell's identity. He would know the name, just as he had known that of Lobetius. Lobetius was another of Walsingham's men.

Walsingham! That name was always cropping up.

He was of course one of the most famous

men in England – a secretary of state, a former ambassador, one of the Queen's privy council – but Martell said his most important role was to run the secret service. Though he was given little money for it he ran the most efficient secret service in Europe.

'He has over fifty agents in his pay,' said Martell, 'in foreign courts and other key positions. I must not tell you names, naturally,' he laughed. 'But you will have guessed that Dr Lobetius is one of them at Strasburg – and Don Gonzalo knows.'

Lobetius had told Martell things last night that had made him eager to press on with his own mission. But first there was the problem of Giles.

'The idea of this tour was mine,' Martell admitted. 'Good cover for my movements from place to place. But it was Walsingham – because he knew your father – who got *you* involved.'

'I'm not blaming anyone.'

'We never meant to bring you into danger. As you were last night. And may be again if you stay with me.'

'I'd like to stay with you.'

'But I promised your parents! I ought to turn round now and take you safely home. It would be only honourable. But I've a higher duty – to Walsingham, to the Queen herself. What

Lobetius told me yesterday makes it doubly vital to get on with my mission. Give Gonzalo the slip – and travel south.'

'Then you must, sir.'

'I suppose I could make some arrangement – use the magic of the Walsingham name – find someone reliable going to London from here, who would guarantee to get you safely back . . .'

'And if I agreed to that, sir . . .' Giles had been growing up, fast, in these few hours. 'It couldn't be arranged in five minutes. You'd lose time for yourself – which might be fatal. You'd have lost cover for your journey. You'd have no pupil. So – I can't agree.'

'You don't think you have a duty to your parents?'

'Yes. But like you I've a higher one – to the Queen, if it's all so important.'

'Judge for yourself.'

Swiftly, but clearly, Martell explained.

Giles knew – everyone did – there had been rumours for a year or two that Philip of Spain meant one day to launch an invasion to force England back into her old Catholic faith. But time passed, nothing happened, and the danger was taken less and less seriously. Last year there had been a report that a fleet of eight hundred ships would sail against England – but nothing had come of it.

Such stories were fit only to frighten children. Where would even the Spaniards muster such a force? And what would Francis Drake be doing about it? The Queen herself dismissed the idea.

Walsingham did not. He battled constantly to persuade her. She thought him a fanatic whose hatred of Spain blinded him to everything else.

'It's money, too, of course,' said Martell.

'Money, sir?'

'She has so little. Men think her mean, but that's unfair.'

Elizabeth had no permanent navy. When warships were needed she had to commission them for a particular operation – and increase their number by adding privateers and armed merchant vessels.

'The Treasury sends money for the men's pay and rations and so on – on a monthly basis. She won't let herself in for three months' expense if she thinks the problem may be settled in two!'

Walsingham thought such economical methods were not going to be adequate. Philip could – and would – build up an overwhelming force to attack England. He would collect allies from all over Europe.

'My task,' said Martell, 'is to find hard evidence that this process is under way. Evidence that Her Majesty will *have* to accept. She is no fool . . .'

'Just economical,' said Giles with a twinkle in his eye.

'Lobetius told me last night – Philip is putting out feelers in all directions. Lobetius is based at Strasburg. He can keep his eyes on the Swiss cantons from there. As you know they are very independent, almost like separate little republics, because of the mountains between. But the Catholic ones are united by their faith. Lobetius says they have agreed to back Philip's enterprise. And let us have no schoolboy jokes,' Martell added swiftly, 'about Swiss galleons sailing through the Straits of Dover!'

'I expect he'd want them as soldiers? Aren't the Swiss famous as fighters?'

'Exactly. However big his fleet he can't just pack it with enough troops to conquer England. And he wouldn't need to. He already has thousands of men lined up against the Dutch in Flanders – just across the water. If his galleons can guarantee them a safe sea-crossing – even for a day or two – he can pour those men into Kent. They'd be in London before most of England knew they'd even landed.'

Giles had lost all trace of a smile. The situation was so convenient for the Spanish king.

Elizabeth, reluctant to spend a penny on defence preparations she could not afford, would let herself be lulled into a fatal sense of false security.

Walsingham must convince her how real the danger was. His agents sent scraps of information from a dozen places. Martell had to find reliable facts that would clinch the matter beyond doubt.

'I can't get them here,' he said emphatically.

'Will you have to go to Spain?' Giles asked. It was not an attractive idea.

The tutor shook his head. 'Sheer suicide. Walsingham says the place is Italy. That's where so much of Philip's help will come from. But it's quite possible for an Englishman to travel in Italy – though some parts are safer than others.' He smiled. 'You may remember in Paris, I took the precaution of going to see the Venetian ambassador and getting us passports for Venice. *Most* convenient. The way things have turned out.'

Chapter Nine

First they must throw Gonzalo off the scent. He would have found out Martell's name and almost certainly identified him as another of Walsingham's men, like Lobetius. But Giles had foiled his obvious intention of searching Martell's belongings while he slept.

'What would he have done about *me*?' Giles asked. 'When he found out I'd be in the room? He'd no chance to drug any drink of mine.'

'If you'd woken up he'd have made sure you didn't interfere! After all, he had another man with him. He is quite ruthless, but he doesn't kill people unnecessarily. He would certainly have avoided killing *me*.'

In the world of spying, Martell explained, it was sensible to leave your adversary alive. If you knew who he was, with luck you might feed him false information which would mislead his masters.

'If you kill him,' said Martell sensibly,

'another man will be appointed in his place. You'll have no idea who he is. You'll have to find out. Quickly! Much easier to stick to the devil you know!'

In the free city of Frankfurt Gonzalo had no more power than themselves. In other places, if they were under Spanish domination, a whisper from him would have been far more dangerous.

The immediate problem was to leave Frankfurt without giving him a clue to their next destination.

Martell wasted no time. 'Pack,' he said.

Travelling so light, they never took long over that. They went downstairs, called for breakfast and settled their reckoning. Martell asked for a man to carry their bags to the house of the well-known local bookseller where Master Etienne was staying. He made no secret of their destination.

Within hours, Giles guessed, that information might reach Gonzalo. But the Spaniard would not be free to walk into the house as though it were a public place. It might be a little while before he discovered that the English couple were not there.

In fact they stayed just long enough to see Etienne and explain that they would not be going back with him to Heidelberg. They were going down to the Rhine now to board one of the craft constantly plying up and down that river. For the benefit of any listeners Martell said that they hoped to cross to England from Amsterdam. Only by the flicker of an eyelid did he warn the printer not to take this as their true intention.

They called a fresh porter for their baggage, and a few hours later, indeed, they were on a vessel heading the opposite way, up river towards Strasburg and the south.

'You know,' Martell murmured, 'I picked up one useful idea in Heidelberg. I think we might become Scotsmen for a while.'

'*Scotsmen*?'

'Johnson said it was so much easier for a Scot to move about Europe than an Englishman. People know almost nothing about Scotland except that it's a separate country – and England's age-old enemy. No one's jealous of Scotland or frightened of her. Philip may not like her being Protestant, but England's sufficient target for now.'

'I've never been in Scotland,' said Giles doubtfully. 'But at least we speak the same language—'

Martell laughed. 'Up to a point!'

'It would be much harder if we had to pretend we were German or Dutch.'

Only their official papers would reveal their

true names and nationality. To innkeepers and strangers generally they could call themselves what they liked. If Gonzalo once lost their scent he would find it hard to catch up with them.

Changing his identity like this brought it home to Giles what a complete transformation had taken place in their circumstances during the past twenty-four hours. The educational journey had become an exciting adventure. He was no longer Martell's pupil but his assistant. He was part now of Sir Francis Walsingham's secret network. A fantastic thought. He thrilled to it.

It was hard to obey his companion's first instruction: go on exactly as before. He was to take the same keen interest in his surroundings, ask questions, make solemn notes of the answers, bury his nose in books. Of course. It was all a necessary part of the pretence. Whatever Martell was teaching him it seldom touched on the subject he was now eager to grasp – the new world he had been plunged into, this world of espionage.

'It's better you don't know more than necessary,' Martell explained.

'Why not?' he demanded, disappointed. 'I swear, I'd never give anything away.'

'I don't doubt your determination. Or your courage. That's what I'm afraid of. These people sometimes have a rough way of asking questions. I would sooner they despised you as an ignorant fool, not worth their trouble.' Giles took his meaning and shuddered. After that he asked no questions. What little he learnt of Martell's activities he picked up by accident.

At least he was taught how to handle and reload the pistol in the hollowed book. Having stumbled on the secret, he had better know how to use it in an emergency. 'It shows that something useful can be found in books,' said Martell drily.

Martell no longer withdrew privately for the laborious composition of a letter in cipher. His more important dispatches to Walsingham had to go that way.

Walsingham, Giles gathered, had a little team of helpers ciphering and deciphering such correspondence, and producing forged documents that looked convincing. This year the economical queen had given him more money for the secret service – not much, admittedly, but more. How lucky, Giles thought, that his father was cheerfully paying for this grand tour! It must mean a considerable saving for Walsingham's funds.

They landed at Strasburg, another of the free imperial cities, standing on an island formed by the branches of a tributary, the Ill, which flowed into the Rhine at this point. Giles guessed that their tour would always have brought them to Strasburg, if only for Martell to meet Lobetius who was normally based here.

Thanks to the fortunate – or perhaps unfortunate? – meeting with him at Frankfurt, this was no longer necessary. Would they press straight on? Martell was anxious to reach Venice but the cover story of an educational tour must be kept up. Being now well clear of Frankfurt, they could relax.

'There can be no invasion of England this summer,' said the tutor reassuringly. 'It will take time to make all the preparations. Though if the Queen is to be persuaded to make counter-preparations, that will take time too.'

Giles was surprised at the ease with which he slipped back into his former role of sightseer. The drama of that night in Frankfurt faded. He was glad to have solved the riddle of Martell's double personality and to feel that he himself was on the fringe of this exciting situation. But there was no sign of the mysterious one-gloved Spaniard, no certainty that they would ever see him again, no worrying sense that they were being pursued or were under observation.

He was interested in the ever-changing scenes of these foreign countries. He would enjoy the two days Martell said they would spend in Strasburg. This was what his father was paying for, and that thought relieved his slightly guilty conscience. Martell too began to behave more like a conscientious tutor, accompanying him as he explored the city. Or was that only an act, to convince anyone who observed them?

The island setting of the old city squeezed it into a tight maze of narrow streets with numerous little bridges across the different arms of river. 'This is Crow Bridge,' said Martell cheerfully. 'When criminals were hanged they used to quarter their bodies and display them here, so it got the name—'

'I can guess,' Giles interrupted hastily.

This was the city, said Martell, where Gutenberg the printer had set up long ago and invented movable type.

They visited the cathedral, built of rose-pink stone. It had a great tower at one corner, with a tall spire rising like a lance against the sky. There was a spiral staircase outside, winding up to a platform at the foot of the spire. They climbed it, pausing to study the view.

Eastwards the Black Forest rolled away, the same Black Forest they had seen at Heidelberg. Only here there were bigger and wilder peaks on the horizon.

They reached the platform breathless. 'Three hundred and thirty steps,' Giles panted. 'I counted.'

'You shall have a tankard when we get down,' said Martell.

The Alsatian beer was cool and refreshing. Giles liked it more than the city's famous delicacy, a pâté of fatted goose-liver, which almost made him sick.

'Drink up,' said Martell. 'We must see the famous astronomical clock. It strikes at midday.'

A crowd had gathered in the south transept of the cathedral. No one came to Strasburg without seeing this wonderful clock. Looking up Giles saw a number of little figures from the Bible. As he stared, trying to identify them, one – unmistakably the Devil – came suddenly to life. He reached out and struck the hour. And as the twelve strokes resounded through the church the other figures began to move, acting the story.

It was quite incredible. Christ was blessing the Apostles. And at the end a cock crowed to signal that Peter had denied his master.

'If only they'd do it all again!' Giles gasped.

'Oh, they can – and will. This time tomorrow. Why not sit down and wait?'

But by noon the next day they were across the Rhine, ambling along the forest road on hired horses, bound for Innsbruck, the capital of the Tyrol.

Giles enjoyed this mode of travel. So did

97

Martell, but he missed the talk with fellow travellers in the coaches they used on other days. One never knew what useful scraps of information – or wild rumour – one might pick up.

'It's not so much the strangers I talk to,' he said, 'it's those I just *listen* to. They imagine an Englishman – or a Scotsman – won't understand a word they say.' Giles never ceased to marvel at his tutor's grasp of different languages. He was alert for the least item worth putting into cipher for Walsingham.

Innsbruck was another fine city he never forgot.

It stood in a high, wide valley, overshadowed by mountains, as at Heidelberg its castle a dominant feature. Built by the Archduke Frederick, known as the 'one with the empty pockets'.

'I don't wonder, sir. Just look at that!' Giles stared up at the golden roof, dazzling against the cloudless sky.

'Oh, that was added by the mighty Maximilian.'

Maximilian was a much-loved nobleman who had brought glory to the city by being elected emperor. They went to see his monument in a church. It was the most famous sight in Innsbruck.

It was a vast marble tomb, designed by the court painter of the time. There was no body in it, for the emperor was buried where he had been born, near Vienna. Instead there was a magnificent statue of him, kneeling in prayer, and his life was depicted in twenty-four marble reliefs. 'What a man!' said the tutor as he explained them. A fighter, a patron of scholars, a writer himself . . . versatile. Round his statue were twenty-eight others, colossal bronze figures, family and friends and ancestors. There were legendary heroes he had specially admired. One, Giles was pleased to see, was the English King Arthur.

After Innsbruck, all his thoughts centred on what lay ahead: the fabulous land of Italy, which his mother had hoped they would not need to enter, because it was a dangerous Catholic country, home of the Pope himself. But it was also the home of so much else – poets and painters, art ancient and modern, astounding architecture. The land of the Romans he had learnt about at school . . . He *could* not miss Italy, having come so far.

'You must teach me some more Italian words,' he said. 'I'm going to forget all that German. Put it out of my head!'

'You're not such a fool,' said Martell quietly.

Giles knew that he was right. Since leaving Sussex his ideas had developed in many directions. He did not know what he was going to

do with his life but he was aware of the possibilities. He would be like his companion, store
all knowledge and experience, which might one
day come in useful.

They had taken places today in a coach. It
was a good road – the Romans had built it long
ago. It crossed the Alps by the lowest and easiest
of their passes. It linked Germany with Italy, the
Mediterranean ports and the world beyond, in
Asia and Africa. It was crowded with wagons
and coaches, riders and strings of packhorses.

Martell knew Venice – of course. He talked
of it with enthusiasm and Giles was all agog.
Though the city itself was several days' journey
distant, they would be in Venetian territory once
they were over the Brenner Pass. The Most
Serene Republic had greatly extended its territory during the last century or two. It had
started, ages ago, as a mere place of refuge from
the barbarians, hidden in the marshes and
lagoons of the Adriatic coast. 'Then it gradually
developed into a great naval power,' said
Martell. 'It still is – it's the bulwark of
Christendom against the Turkish fleet.'

It developed also on its landward side. To
meet the threat of Milan, which was coming
to dominate much of northern Italy, cities like
Verona and Padua merged with the Serenissima.
The Venetian emblem – a lion with wings –

would greet them as soon as they were south of the Alps.

The Brenner Pass proved no obstacle. It was just a broad, flattish stretch of ground between sloping pinewoods. Two days more, and they were boarding the ferry-boat to the clustered towers and domes glittering across the lagoon.

Within an hour or two they had complied with the official formalities and found lodgings near an arched bridge called the Rialto. A servant humped their baggage up a lot of stairs. Giles almost ran across the tiled floor to the sun-drenched balcony beyond.

Leaning over the balustrade he looked down on green water, lined on both sides with equally tall buildings. Slim black boats were gliding to and fro, propelled by confident gondoliers, standing like statues, with single oars which they wielded with expert skill.

This must be the Grand Canal. He turned to Martell. '*Venice*!' he whispered, husky with delight.

'You didn't think I'd lose you?' said his friend.

Chapter Ten

In Venice everything was different.

It was not just that there were rippling waterways instead of paved streets. In fact you could get around the city quite well on foot, thanks to the innumerable little bridges, the overshadowed squares as tiny as courtyards, and the narrow alleys that did not wind but turned at sudden right angles shaped by the tall houses that hung over them.

Even the food was different. The Italians cooked in olive oil. They served unfamiliar dishes which, Martell explained, they had brought in from Asia or North Africa. The Venetians especially were such travellers, with trading contacts everywhere.

They had taken up, too, strange fruits and vegetables that Spain had found in the new world of America. Now, some of them were grown widely in the similar climate of Italy.

'Have another of these,' said Martell,

offering Giles a bowl of glossy little red globes that were soft and juicy when you bit into their greeny-gold insides. 'The Spaniards called them love-apples when they first met them.'

'Why? Apples are firmer – and sweeter. And why "love"?'

Martell laughed. 'They thought that eating them made you a more passionate lover. You'd better not overdo them. You're getting to that age!'

The Mexican word for them was *tomatl* and it had been adopted by the Spaniards and Italians. These tomatoes could be cooked or eaten raw. Giles liked them, but could not see how they would affect his private life as things were at present.

Martell became again the conscientious tutor. They showed themselves everywhere, touring the famous sights – the Doges' palace and St Mark's with its five domes, palaces and churches innumerable, old and new like San Giorgo Maggiore, which had a little islet all to itself.

The famous architect Palladio had been rebuilding it when he died a few years ago. 'That man was tireless,' said Martell. 'We'll be seeing his work everywhere!'

There was so much to see. Paintings by Titian and countless other artists. Frescoes, painted on walls, a complete novelty to Giles. Superb statues like the one of the soldier of fortune, Colleoni, on horseback. Martell told exciting stories of his adventures and escapes.

Sometimes, as before, the tutor would quietly slip away without explanation. Giles never asked for one. He knew that Walsingham had a permanent agent in Venice, as in many cities, but these local men seldom risked behaving as actual spies. Martell never forgot why he was there. He was making contacts, listening, gathering every possible scrap of information. Was Venice really getting involved with Philip's plot against England?

He did not like to think it. Her relations with England were normally friendly; their interests did not clash. Though Catholics, the Venetians were so jealous of their independence that they would not meekly take orders from Rome. The Holy Office – the Inquisition – was not allowed to use the same severity it showed in other countries. It did not have its own prison for offenders. Each doge, on election, promised to burn heretics alive, but no one ever did.

They might burn a dead body – or even a dummy – but never a living man. Some years ago a pope had decreed that universities should not give degrees to non-Catholics. Venice had no university of her own, but the oldest university in Italy was in her allied city of Padua. Padua stubbornly continued to treat all students alike. Encouraged by the Venetian Senate she gave degrees to all who earned them, whatever their religion.

'I think we are safer here than anywhere else in Italy,' said Martell.

True, he admitted, there were the Inquisitors of State, an official department as efficient as most government departments were in this republic. Others dredged the canals and removed barge-loads of filth and rubbish, burnt aromatic spices to offset the smells and shipped clean drinking water from the mainland.

'The Inquisitors are particularly hot on spies,' he said.

'We'd better be careful then!'

'I have been.' Martell smiled. 'I have made a friend. He told me – as I was a Scotsman! – that there was a conspiracy brewing against England.'

'Did he say what Venice—'

'No, we must find out for ourselves.'

He bought Giles a big notebook such as artists used. It would look well if he sketched some buildings. It was a suitable thing for a student to do. It would leave his tutor to stroll about and strike up conversations with strangers.

'A good cover,' said Giles. He was handy with a pencil and he would like to give Olivia an idea of the wonders he had seen.

At first he chose obvious subjects like the ancient Rialto bridge with its drawbridge in the middle that opened to let large craft pass. On the third day Martell headed for the shabbier quarter of the Castello.

'There are rich and poor in Venice, like everywhere else,' he said. 'These men are dock-yard workers. Their wives and daughters work even harder, stitching the sails. The women earn only twelve ducats a year – less than a novice shipwright.'

'Why are we—' Giles began.

'I want you to sketch *this*,' said Martell.

Giles tried to hide his dismay. Facing them was a long stretch of high blank wall, featureless except for battlements like an endless row of teeth. The dullest subject imaginable.

'The Arsenal,' went on his tutor. 'All the galleys are built, repaired and fitted out here. There's a basin behind that wall. Eighty acres of water. Sixteen thousand men are employed here.'

Giles saw a ray of hope. 'Won't it be suspicious if I sit down and start sketching? Won't they think I'm a spy? A naval place like this . . .'

'They're not afraid. No one could touch the Arsenal. It would take a foreign army with siege-engines and cannon. How would you get them into the middle of Venice? They're used to artists. If we walk on you'll see the great entrance gate – it's a work of art itself. People often draw and paint it.'

When they reached it Giles was suitably impressed. It might not appeal to his sister but it was more interesting than the battlements. He found a patch of shade and started work. Martell explained that it was the only entrance gate to the whole vast site, closely guarded and subject to the strictest regulations.

Then he strolled off, with the air of a teacher who had settled his pupil to a task and must now fill in an hour or two as best he could. The sketchbook was proving a useful alibi.

Plenty of people were about. Several, because Giles was young, felt free to stop, peer over his shoulder and comment. There was a French gentleman he could answer fluently, a German not so well. The local men, retired shipwrights he guessed, were hardest of all. They did not speak the sort of Italian Martell was trying to teach him, but a Venetian dialect that baffled even his tutor.

Once the shuffling footsteps paused, and a voice behind him quavered: 'Verra guid, laddie! Verra guid!'

Giles turned and looked into a wrinkled face

with wisps of sandy hair escaping from beneath the hat. 'Thank you, sir.'

'You'd be the Scots lad I've heerd of? Drawin' pictures?'

My accent, Giles thought with dismay. But he dared not try to imitate the Scotsman. 'My mother was English,' he said truthfully.

Luckily the old gentleman seemed more than ready to do most of the talking. He had been away from Scotland so long – he lived chiefly in Rome now – and it was fine to meet someone from his home country.

When first adopting the Scottish pretence Giles had invented an imaginary background for himself. He had grown up in a quiet country home, vaguely – very vaguely – near Edinburgh, and had seen little of Scotland. 'Tell as few lies as possible,' Martell had advised him, 'then there's less risk of being caught out.' He would be wise to switch any conversation to personal questions, simply transferring (with obvious adjustments) his Sussex life to the Lowlands. 'Talk about your horse – and your sister. By her real name. If you change that you're sure to make a slip.'

Luckily the genuine Scotsman accepted the excuse for his lack of Scottish accent. He would lose his own if he spent many more years here talking Latin and Italian and other languages.

He had hoped . . . but hopes of going back had faded now with the queen's death.

Giles was startled by this, then realized that he meant the recently executed Queen of Scots. 'God rest her soul,' the old man added. His hands trembled as he made the sign of the cross.

I'd better be careful, Giles thought.

Of course! Just as there were English Catholics living in Rome so there must be Scotsmen who preferred exile to the strict Protestant regime of their own country.

Fortunately the old man changed the subject. 'Ye've found guid quarters in Venice? Which inn—'

'No inn, sir. My tutor knew of some excellent lodgings. Near the Rialto. Overlooking the Grand Canal.' Giles bit his lip. Perhaps a mistake to give even that much away? He bent over his sketchbook and concentrated on the elaborate gateway.

The man went rambling on over his head. Or *was* he just rambling? Once or twice he sounded almost as though he were probing. Giles became desperately evasive but hoped it did not show.

'There are grand views across the water in Venice, laddie, but to my mind nothing to match the sunsets at Edinburgh – the sun goin' doon into the Clyde . . .'

'Indeed no, sir,' Giles agreed with polite enthusiasm.

In the distance he saw Martell coming back. In one way it was a relief. In another it might be awkward if his tutor said something that contradicted a remark of his own. To his relief the stranger said, almost abruptly: 'It's late. I mun gang on my way. A good picture, laddie. Carry on wi' it.' He had vanished round a corner long before Martell reached Giles.

'So *you've* had an encounter with the talk-ative Scot?' The tutor's bantering tone had a faint tinge of anxiety.

'You know him, sir?'

'He fastened on to me half an hour ago. Rather inquisitive – didn't you find him so? I fear I was a disappointment.'

'I was careful not to give anything away.' Giles hoped that his mention of their lodgings had been harmlessly vague. 'He did most of the talking. General things. Like the beautiful views from Edinburgh, over the Clyde . . .'

'The *Clyde*?' Martell looked suddenly alarmed.

'That's what he said.'

'The Clyde's on the other side of Scotland! At Edinburgh you look across the Firth of Forth.'

'Perhaps *he's* only pretending to be a

110

Scotsman?' Giles knew that he was clutching at the feeblest hope.

'And perhaps he was testing if *you* were?' said Martell grimly.

They both knew that was more probable. In panic Giles thought back over the conversation. His own accent, his occasional slowness in grasping what the old man was saying . . . No wonder suspicion had been aroused! If the man *was* a Catholic living in Rome he might have contacts that could be dangerous.

He was relieved that his tutor did not explode in anger. Fortunately Martell had himself had a profitable morning, gossiping with other strangers in a tavern. He had found confirmation of a rumour that had brought him to Venice. Behind those walls the Arsenal was humming with activity.

'Venice has promised dozens of war galleys for an expedition,' he said. 'Against England.'

Chapter Eleven

Only yesterday Giles had admired one of the galleys crossing the lagoon. So elegant, so long and slender, its oars flashing in the sun. It was hard to imagine such craft battling with the Atlantic rollers as they made for England. The ocean surely called for the square-rigged vessels in which men like Drake swept the Spanish Main?

Martell corrected him as they walked. Those three-masted galleys carried a good spread of canvas and in calm weather the oarsmen gave them an extra advantage. As for coping with the Atlantic – well, there was a regular service of trading galleys between Southampton and the Adriatic port of Otranto. They reckoned to do the trip in a month, two to three thousand miles.

One of the men he had talked to said that Genoa, Italy's other naval power, had joined the Spanish plan. Between them the two republics were contributing eighty galleys. With all the

Spanish galleons – and those of Portugal, where Philip had recently seized the vacant throne – the expedition would have overwhelming strength.

'But it cannot be ready this summer,' said Martell.

This visit to the Arsenal neighbourhood had paid off. Talking to local people he had picked up details he would never have learnt from chance conversations on the Rialto or the great piazza of St Mark.

'Venice has to import timber now for big vessels. They've used up the good local oak they relied on years ago.'

Only the Scottish stranger troubled him. Luckily Martell had a good general knowledge of Scotland. As he was already talking to several Italians outside the tavern when the man joined them, the conversation had continued in their language. They had exchanged hardly a word of English.

'Sorry now that I mentioned *you*. But your sketching was my excuse for being there, with time on my hands.'

Was there anything sinister in the Scotsman's later making a bee-line for Giles and apparently trapping him with that reference to the Clyde? Would he now report his suspicions? The Venetian Inquisitors of State might submit them to awkward questioning.

'I'd have liked to stay here longer,' said Martell. 'But better be on the safe side.'

They could move to Padua. It was near and had excellent communications with Venice. Its ancient university was full of young foreigners. Giles could lose himself among them. Martell could maintain his secret Venetian contacts.

It would be too obvious, though, if they immediately settled in Padua. Subtler to pass it by, take another route, and after a few days approach Padua from the opposite direction.

Giles felt sad to be leaving Venice so soon. 'You'll see Venice again,' said Martell. 'Sure to.'

How soon, and in what nerve-racking circumstances, neither of them could have guessed.

There were compensations, however. For two reasons Giles was always thankful to have visited Vicenza.

For one thing it was the home town of that architect, Andrea Palladio, whose name and work had been constantly with him in those first days in Italy. Palladio had been inspired by the ancient Greeks and Romans and had changed the trend of fashion. He had worked in many places but he had really set his mark on Vicenza. When they arrived on their second day – after a roundabout journey to avoid Padua – they had been amazed by the number of new mansions and villas he had built in this smallish city.

The second thing was meeting Peppina Niccolini.

That was the next morning. After a stroll round with Martell he had settled down to sketch the Teatro Olimpico – perhaps the most interesting and most novel of Palladio's works, a permanent building for the performance of plays. There was nothing like it in England, probably nothing in the whole world.

He was so absorbed that he was unaware of her existence until he picked up a new, fragrant scent and turned his head sharply to see where it came from. Their faces almost collided, for in her eagerness to see his sketch her chin was just above his shoulder. These Italian girls wore smaller ruffs than the English.

He sprang up, startled. And the girl sprang back with a stream of confused apology. He understood only: 'You are drawing my uncle's theatre!' She sounded delighted.

That broke the ice. 'Palladio was your uncle?'

She nodded vigorously. She was very pretty. Dark-haired and golden-skinned, delicate of feature, not tall – petite really – but probably about his own age.

He had to explain that he was English, travelling with a tutor, and her eyes widened with interest. Martell had decided for the present to drop the Scottish pretence – if the old Scotsman had set anyone on their trail it would be more of a danger than a disguise. The girl, surprisingly, tried Latin and they were able to talk more easily.

'You must not think me shameless,' she said, 'speaking to a strange young man! But when I saw you drawing the theatre I was so proud – I forgot decorum . . .'

'And Palladio was really your uncle?'

'Some distant sort of cousin, actually – we worked it out once – but he was an old man, so "Uncle Andrea" sounded more respectful.'

Giles was fascinated. And not only by her connection with the famous architect.

She was peering at the drawing. 'This is good. But have you been inside? Oh, you *must*. The stage – everything!'

She was compelling. He followed her meekly to the entrance. But there even her charm failed. A man barred their path. No one could go in.

'There is a rehearsal in progress, *signorina*.'

She stamped her foot and turned apologetically to Giles. 'Of course! That is why my father has brought me over from Padua. It is so seldom there is a performance.'

Small as the city was it had a select little academy of people who cared about the arts. They had commissioned this building from her

Uncle Andrea and tonight there was a repeat of the play with which it had opened several years before. An ancient Greek tragedy, *King Oedipus*, by Sophocles.

'All the best people will be here. It will be packed. You should come!'

'But if—'

'My father will get you in. He is a leading bookseller in Padua. You and your tutor will be distinguished foreign visitors.' She bubbled with confidence.

They saw Martell waiting at the spot where he had left Giles sketching. Giles introduced them a little nervously. Martell always got anxious lest his pupil should forget that nations varied in manners and a free-and-easy English boy could give offence, especially when talking to girls.

Martell however seemed relaxed. If the young lady's father approved . . . so kind a gesture would be much appreciated . . .

They found Signor Niccolini at the inn where he and his daughter were staying. It was Martell's turn to use his charm.

He mentioned their visit to the Frankfurt book fair – but not their dramatic experience there. He referred casually to his friend Sir Francis Walsingham. Giles caught his breath. Wasn't that terribly unwise, indeed dangerous?

But the good effect on the bookseller reassured him. Niccolini remembered the days when English students flocked to Padua. Walsingham had been oustanding among them.

'He was chosen Consularius of the English Nation in the Faculty of Civil Law.' The bookseller rolled the title round his tongue. 'He would only be my age. About twenty-three. He often came into our shop.'

People in Padua remembered him. Some knew he had gone on to a brilliant career. An ambassador. Prominent in Queen Elizabeth's council. But no one here, Giles guessed, knew of his other work, running her secret service.

Niccolini was clearly much impressed by Martell. There was no problem about conjuring up two seats for the theatre.

The English couple could not compete with the fashionable splendours of the assembly they encountered there. Peppina had abandoned the shortish skirt which revealed her darting little feet. ('Why should *I* sweep the street when we have men with brooms?') Now her long rustling gown did sweep the floor. She wore red satin, embroidered in gold, with silver buttons. She looked, thought Giles, as fine as the theatre itself.

No wonder she had been keen to show him the interior. The wide stage was backed by a permanent wall of crowded classical sculpture, pierced by an archway and lesser openings to right and left. Each of these revealed a street with buildings stretching apparently into the distance. But that was only an optical illusion. The buildings were solid enough but diminished rapidly in size and actors had only a few paces to walk for their exit.

There were two more exits, adorned with statues, at the sides. More statues, a double row, curved round the auditorium. The audience sat on backless stone seats, rising in semicircular tiers. As they settled themselves in their places Peppina whispered, 'What a feast for the eye! Though,' she added mischievously, 'a little hard on the bottom.' Giles soon agreed.

He had scarcely seen a play himself, only entertainments put on by touring troupes of actors driven out of London by plague. *King Oedipus*, written two thousand years ago, was very different from those.

The original Greek had been translated into Italian. Peppina's whispers gave him the gist. There was music commissioned from Andrea Gabrieli, a rising young composer in Venice, for the first performance. The superb costumes designed for that occasion had been brought out again. Altogether an unforgettable experience.

'You made a great impression yourself, sir,' Giles assured Martell. 'All those grand people we were introduced to! They were all calling you "doctor"!'

Martell laughed. 'They call everyone *dottore* in Italy if he seems reasonably well educated. Just to be on the safe side. But it has been a profitable evening.'

'Profitable?'

'When Signor Niccolini heard we were planning to travel to Padua he invited us to stay with them.'

Giles tried to conceal his delight. 'Did you accept?'

'Yes. If, of course' – Martell was almost grinning – 'that is agreeable to *you*.'

Chapter Twelve

Teasing him, Martell justified the arrangement as though he were reporting it in code to Walsingham.

'It will have the advantage that we arrive in Padua not as unknown foreigners but as guests of a prominent citizen. No one will question our identity or our motives. And staying in a private house we shall not be exposed to prying strangers.' He added slyly, 'There may be other attractions, if I could think of them.'

'I could,' said Giles. But imitating Martell's previous tone he went on wickedly, 'We shall save on food and lodging – an economy for the privy purse.'

Later the tutor once more emphasized the importance of care in his behaviour towards foreign girls. Italians who visited England were shocked by the free and easy kissing there . . .

'There'll be nothing like that,' said Giles gravely. He knew that Italian fathers and

121

brothers did not like one to take such liberties. 'I don't want to die in a dark alley!'

They travelled next morning in a comfortable coach with Peppina and her father and their Paduan friends. The twenty-mile journey took under three hours.

Palladio had been a Paduan, but had fled at thirteen from the carpenter to whom he was apprenticed. Vicenza became his adopted city.

'He was an independent lad,' said Signor Niccolini.

'Like you, I imagine,' Peppina whispered.

Padua's massive walls encircled a city bigger than Vicenza. Inside, it was divided by the various branches of a winding river.

The Niccolinis' house looked down on one of these. They no longer lived over their bookshop, but close by. Antonio and Paolo, Peppina's brothers, were still at home, now with wives and families. 'Everywhere,' she warned Giles, 'you'll find small children underfoot.'

They entered through an impressive vaulted portico. There were two marble-paved galleries and a colonnaded gallery. Upstairs they met Signora Niccolini in a fine room where she had been sitting at a window, studying the passersby. She gave them a warm welcome and was quite unflurried by her unexpected guests. She had plenty of servants.

There were carpets and tapestries everywhere, chests and cupboards in their bedroom,
soft and springy beds. Summoned to the evening
meal, they found the family assembling in a
pleasant dining room with a door open to the
garden and a gleam of green river beyond. A
maid came round with a ewer of warm water so
that they could all wash their hands. Then the
bookseller murmured a Latin grace and they sat
down, Martell in the place of honour on the
signora's right, Giles on her left, with Peppina
on his other side.

It was a good meal. It started with slices of
melon and went on to a varied choice of roast
chicken, trout, veal, sausages and stew, all of
which Giles was urged to try.

They finished with fruit.

Conversation had to be mainly in Italian,
with Peppina and her father interpreting.
Neither her mother nor the sisters-in-law spoke
any other language. Antonio was fluent in
French.

'Have you met a young Scots boy?' he
enquired. 'Travelling with a tutor? Like you . . .'

'No,' said Giles, as lightly as possible. 'Why?'

'I just thought – speaking the same language – you would be able to exchange
impressions . . .'

'What are they like?'

'I have not seen them. But yesterday morning a customer was enquiring for them. He thought they might be in Padua, and would visit a famous shop like ours.'

Martell joined in the conversation. 'What was *he* like?'

'The customer?' Antonio hesitated. 'I hardly remember – the shop was so busy. I think what struck me was that he did not seem particularly interested in the books. He glanced at them, but did not even take off his gloves to turn the pages.'

Giles took care not to look at his tutor.

'We had only the briefest conversation,' Antonio went on. 'He said he must be mistaken. He had already tried the obvious inns. No one had seen a couple answering to his description. They could not have come to Padua after all. I think,' Antonio concluded, 'he was a Spaniard himself.'

Giles could not speak to Martell until they were preparing for bed.

'What luck that we didn't come straight to Padua!'

'Not luck. An obvious precaution.'

The old Scotsman must, as they had feared, have reported his suspicions to someone. It was probably pure chance that Gonzalo was by then in Venice, but being there he was just the sort

124

of person to hear of that report – and link it with the couple he had met in Frankfurt.

'It is good luck for us,' said Martell. 'He will have crossed Padua off his list.'

Giles was not entirely happy to know that this sinister character was still taking such an interest in them.

As Martell had hoped, this spell in Padua proved convenient for his own enquiries. He could make contact with Walsingham's agent in Venice. Signor Niccolini had business correspondence all over Europe and would slip mail into his postbag for London. And his bookshop was a Mecca for travellers passing through Padua.

It was a pool, said Martell, where he could fish for information. Better than sitting in taverns, drinking more than he wanted, in the hope of striking up useful conversations. He spent congenial hours, dipping into the books with genuine enjoyment, but eyes and ears always alert for some other browsing customer who might have just arrived from Rome, say, with the latest political gossip.

The rumour of a possible attack on England cropped up constantly, sometimes in the most indirect way. A Frenchman, for instance, mentioned a Spaniard who wrote plays. This man, like Gonzalo, had been wounded at Lepanto and forced to find a new livelihood. 'His plays are good enough, but the pay is contemptible,' said the Frenchman. 'He would do better to write books.' The hapless playwright was now reduced to a humdrum job for the Spanish government, arranging wheat supplies to provision some fantastic naval expedition. His name, Cervantes, came back to Giles many years later, on the title page of a book called *Don Quixote*.

Martell did not haunt the bookshop all day. His reputation as a man of learning spread through the university and *il dottore* Martell was welcome in many circles. Years ago the English had been numerous there. Henry VIII's cousin had come on from Oxford. Later there had been Walsingham and other Englishmen, afterwards famous. Elderly men remembered those days and were sorry that political events had reduced the flow from England.

'Many of them dislike the Spaniards,' he reported. 'They quite like hearing about Drake and his raid on Cadiz. They've no love for King Philip – but of course, if the Pope says the English are wicked heretics, it's a different matter.'

Even Martell, dogged and patient though he was, got depressed by the slow progress of his mission.

'What we want,' he told Giles, 'is something *big*. Something definite, that will really convince Her Majesty. I fancy that Sir Francis is almost at his wits' end. She doesn't *want* to believe in this armada – she can't face the huge expense of preparing against it. She shuts her eyes. And she is not a woman to argue with. Poor Walsingham struggles on, but he must find evidence she can't ignore.'

What hope was there, Giles wondered, of picking up that sort of evidence? Apart from that frustration he himself was vastly enjoying his stay in Padua.

They had to keep up the deception, of course, tutor and pupil, though Martell needed all his time for his real work. They found ways to set him free. Giles went to lectures – and was supposed to write essays on them to discuss with his conscientious companion. The sketchbook came out again. He might be seen sketching buildings all over the city. Obviously there was much that the boy could do on his own.

Only Giles was seldom on his own.

'I thought it best,' Martell explained to people, 'that he should be taken round Padua by a native. So, very kindly, Signor Niccolini has told his daughter . . .' Peppina had not needed telling.

She was glad of the excuse to escape the

endless embroidery and household occupations of her home. She had inherited her father's love of books – even more than her brothers, who sold them. Her sisters-in-law cared nothing for them. She had few interests in common with them.

'Why shouldn't women be as well-read as men?' she would ask them furiously. 'My father says—'

'Naturally,' they would answer, laughing, 'he's a bookseller – it increases his sales.'

She and Giles would discuss opinions and enthusiasms as she led him round Padua. She showed him the Byzantine-style basilica of San Antonio with its six domes and its two bell towers like eastern minarets. He liked wall-paintings? She took him to the chapel with Giotto's famous frescoes of scenes from the Bible. He must see the splendid horseback statue of Gattamelata, the first great bronze to be cast in Italy. How did it compare with the statue of Colleone, which he'd seen in Venice?

More than once they went to the Botanical Garden, also the first in Italy, where students could study plants and trees. The first trees planted were now tall and cast welcome shade where other young people could sit and talk.

Giles found her talk fascinating – he was getting more fluent in Italian, but they could

128

turn to Latin if they got stuck. Her views on women's freedom were startling. Where did she get them?

'When I was a little girl I did not only *dust* the books in the shop,' she said. 'Gelli – a Florentine – for instance.' She quoted. 'Husbands "regard women as slaves and servants – this is so contrary to the natural order of things, no other animal than man has the audacity." And Bandello, who wrote splendid stories like *The Duchess of Malfi* . . .' She forgot that no English boy would have read it. 'Bandello said wives should have decent liberty.'

He knew that such notions would have shocked many people at home, but knowing Peppina – and remembering Olivia – he agreed.

She was scornful of make-up though she loved a subtle and alluring scent. Her sisters-in-law warned her not to despise beauty aids. 'Wait till you're a bit older, though,' they warned her darkly. 'Then you'll realize.'

'I'm not going to rub my hands with a mixture of mustard and apple and bitter almonds,' she said, 'and then wear tight chamois leather gloves in bed to keep them soft and white!'

However, 'Cleanliness is what matters,' she said firmly. A well-bred woman should have an all-over wash every day, in clean pumped water that fragrant herbs had been boiled in. Giles saw how highly cleanliness was regarded in her home. Every Saturday his own bed-linen was whisked away and changed.

They got to know each other very well on those walks. He discovered that Peppina was already engaged – to a young man, son of a business friend of her father's in Venice. He was prepared for that. Peppina's marriage was sure to be arranged for her. An Italian, a Catholic of course. But Niccolini would have chosen someone likely to make her happy.

They had passed on to talk of other things. It was half an hour later that the girl said suddenly, 'What a *pity*, Giles, that you are a heretic!' Nothing more was said. There was no more that could be.

Some evenings later, Martell told Giles, 'Tomorrow morning I must leave you – only for a few days.'

'Leave me? Why? Where are you going?'

'Rome.'

The name struck a chill. Rome spelt danger. The one place they had meant to avoid. Nowadays it could be a death-trap to Englishmen, unless they were Catholic exiles. Others took a chance – but it was a chance.

Martell read his thoughts. 'Yes, there *are* certain risks. Luckily this is the ideal place to leave you. You are safe with the Niccolinis. You have your lectures and' – he smiled – 'I have delegated your artistic education to the most competent signorina.'

'Must you go to Rome, sir?'

'I must. I learnt something today. The Spanish ambassador is to have important conversations with the Holy Father. It may give me the sort of news that will really convince the Queen of her danger – the whole country's danger.'

The last thing Giles wanted was to leave Padua. But he said, with complete determination, 'And what about *your* danger, sir? If you go to Rome I'm going with you.'

Chapter Thirteen

Martell argued. He had to think of his pupil's safety, his responsibility to the parents. When Giles brushed this aside he suggested – unfairly, Giles thought – that his company might be more of a handicap than a help.

'Like that night in Frankfurt?' Giles retorted.

Martell instantly apologized. 'I'll never cease to be grateful for what you did. But if Gonzalo hears that an English – or Scottish – boy has turned up in Rome with his tutor, he'll be curious. He may be in Rome himself by now. He moves about.'

Giles saw the force of the argument. The teacher-pupil pretence had served its purpose as a cloak for Martell's activities. Now it might give him away.

'Let's change places – alter the relationship,' he suggested. 'You become the grand tourist. I'll be your servant.'

In the end Martell gave way. There were of

course a number of Englishmen living in Rome, Catholic exiles hoping for the day when the old religion would be restored in their own country. The head of this group was a Cardinal William Allen, already designated the next Archbishop of Canterbury when that day came. Other Englishmen turning up in the city were suspected as heretics and possible spies. They risked death or torture. Cardinal Allen was adopting a more reasonable attitude. If these strangers only wanted to see the sights of Rome, he turned a blind eye. They could come and go without interference.

Martell must go as such a tourist. If he had a servant he would look more like a genuine gentleman than if he were quite alone.

They made their excuses to the Niccolinis that evening. Peppina looked sad and urged them to come back via Padua. Giles had a bitter secret thought that they would not. If Martell got his vital evidence he would make straight for England.

They soon crossed the frontier into the Papal States. These stretched halfway down the Italian peninsula to Rome itself. Impatient though he was, Martell forced himself to keep to a reasonable pace. 'We mustn't gallop as though we were king's messengers.'

Sometimes he made a zigzag detour. This, he

said, was not to throw off pursuers – he did not think anyone was following them. It was to avoid towns where there was an outbreak of plague. 'It would ruin everything,' he explained, 'if we were shut out of Rome because we hadn't a clean bill of health.'

Tiresome though it was, they took a week to reach their destination. They had to keep to main roads to get a change of horses at the post-houses. But it was a safer countryside than when Martell had had to slip through it a few years earlier.

'The Pope's territories were in chaos then. Brigands! Huge bands of them, organized in hundreds, terrorizing everybody.'

In the last two years the new Pope, Sixtus the Fifth, had cleaned them up – mercilessly. It had been reckoned that there had been twenty-seven thousand of them. Not now.

'He's a strong man, I'll give him that. He's going to restore Rome to its old glory. He's put up the taxes – but people pay. He says he's building up treasure to fight the Turks and the heretics. Everywhere!'

'Including the English?'

'That's what King Philip wants to know. So do I.'

This Pope had found Rome a city of wretchedness and misery. Giles found it a city of chaos

134

– but of hope. Demolition and rebuilding every-where. Whole streets swept away, whole tracts of slums. Armies of workmen.

The tops of the famous seven hills were being cleared for fine new buildings – especially the Esquiline and the Viminal and the Quirinal, where Sixtus planned a new palace for himself. There was to be a new aqueduct. He restarted work on the great dome Michelangelo had designed for St Peter's. He took down an obelisk in the Circus Neronis and set it up facing that church. He took down statues of ancient emperors and put apostles in their places.

'I wonder you can still find your way about,' Giles said.

'I shall need to,' said Martell grimly.

Luckily no one had demolished the 'safe house' he knew of, on the northern side of the city, and they were soon established there in a side-turning near the Via Flaminia.

The house was clean, quiet and convenient for their purpose, kept by a decent old woman who was deaf and spoke only Italian. She provided no meals. They used various eating-houses in the neighbourhood, never the same one, so that they would not become familiar figures at any. They seldom saw the other lodgers, who seemed respectable enough and birds of passage like themselves.

'She can be trusted absolutely,' said Martell. 'She has no love for the authorities.' He paused. 'Her husband died a terrible death at their hands. Quite unjustly.'

Her staff consisted of a giggling grand-daughter, and a limping dim-sighted old man who acted as porter.

Rome, Giles decided, looked like providing the dullest part of his grand tour. Martell, as usual, made his own programme and did not discuss it unnecessarily. Away from their lodgings there was no point in revealing their connection.

'One thing you can do for me,' said Martell, 'is shadow me for a little while when I start out in the mornings.'

'Shadow you?'

'Just to make sure I have no other shadow.'

Giles must not follow him too closely. If any one were watching the house the manoeuvre would be obvious. So Giles would follow after a few minutes, making for a little street-market they had noticed a short distance away. Martell would be studying the fruit stalls. They would not show any sign of recognition and Giles would keep in the background, observing whether any stranger seemed to be taking a special interest in his tutor – and particularly, when Martell moved on, if anyone immediately followed in the same direction.

Martell would find reasons to pause frequently. Each pause would help to confirm whether he had a shadow. After three or four such halts Giles would overtake Martell and murmur, in passing, either a warning or an assurance that all seemed well.

After several days of this, Martell felt confident that no one had traced him here. Giles could start a lonely day of sightseeing, identifying the famous landmarks as best he could – not easy amid the present flurry of reconstruction. No Martell, no Peppina. Unwise to use even helpful strangers, since to open his mouth would betray his nationality. He had to rack his brain for schoolday recollections of Julius Caesar and the poems of Horace and the amphitheatre where Nero had loosed the lions on the Christian martyrs. The huge ruins of that building he could identify. He would have liked to write home and to Peppina but knew it would be better not to.

Martell sometimes did not come back to their lodgings until late. His spirits varied. Giles could only speculate on how his day had gone. Had he managed to make contact with anyone on the Pope's staff? That would be safer than approaching any of the Spanish ambassador's followers. Though Martell, in his desperation, might risk attempting both.

A papal contact seemed more likely. Martell talked a lot about Sixtus – and with great respect. Sixtus was a formidable man. He was said to admire the English queen and to declare that, if she were not a heretic, she would be his most beloved princess in Europe. He had startled the Spanish ambassador by losing his temper and throwing the plates about the room. Apparently he quite often did this.

It certainly sounded as though Martell had been talking to someone near the centre of these vital discussions.

One evening Martell was unusually late. Giles decided he could keep awake no longer. He knew Martell too well now to be seriously worried. If he was on the track of worthwhile information he would stay out all night to get it. If he came back in the small hours he would bang on the shutters below and the old man would unbolt the door.

Some sound woke Giles earlier than usual. The beginnings of dawn cast just enough pale grey light to show that Martell's bed was empty. Even now he felt no great concern, he had such confidence in the man. He was about to roll over for another hour or two's sleep when he heard again the voices which must have roused him. Familiar voices.

'Stand aside from that door,' said Martell quietly.

'I think not.' That was Gonzalo. The Spaniard's suave voice came back to him. They were speaking in Italian, but their brief exchange was clear enough.

'What do you want? You have been following me.'

'I want – I must have – your silence.'

'On what?'

'On whatever you have learnt tonight.'

They must be standing just under the window, Gonzalo barring Martell's way to the door below. Giles was by now out of bed, seizing that hollowed volume Martell kept under his pillow, silently drawing out the loaded pistol. Thank God that Martell had long ago instructed him, even given him a little target practice at a lonely stopping-place when they rode across the Alps. He crept now to the open casement and peeped down.

Both men had drawn their rapiers. Was the story of Gonzalo's injured hand just a legend, the mysterious single glove a trick to make an opponent over-confident? Giles caught his breath.

'And there is only one way to ensure your silence,' the Spaniard went on smoothly.

Giles felt a terrible indecision. Should he shout – or shoot? There was no time to clatter down those stairs and open the door.

In that moment of hesitation he saw the third man. A stealthy shadow creeping forward out of the gloom, step by step, behind Martell's back. Gonzalo could see him, of course. He was holding Martell's attention while his unknown companion drew close enough to plunge that upraised dagger between his shoulderblades.

No time for indecision now. Giles thrust out his arm, slanting down over the windowsill, and pulled the trigger. There was a spurt of fire, a bang that set the pigeons whirling round the rooftops, a howl of pain from Gonzalo's companion. The dagger clattered on the paving stones.

No time for the fumbling business of reloading. Giles thundered down the stairs, yanked back the door bolts and burst into the street.

Martell was already alone, stooping to pick up Gonzalo's rapier. Racing footsteps faded in the distance.

'Good work!' he said. 'He'd hoped to trick me with his sword – hold my attention while his man crept up behind me. His crippled hand is genuine enough. When our blades crossed I sent his flying from his hand. Your pistol scared him, too. He wouldn't know how many of you there were.'

'He'll come back!'

'Be sure he will. He mustn't find us here. And he needn't.' Martell's voice had an exultant ring. 'I got all I wanted for Walsingham last night. And Gonzalo knows I did. So he must silence me before I pass it on.'

'And now . . .?'

'It's England now. Quick as we can.'

Chapter Fourteen

An odd pistol-shot at dawn seemed to attract little notice in this rather shabby quarter. No other doors opened, no faces appeared at windows, no one shouted.

They hurried inside and shot the bolts. Their few belongings took little time to pack. Giles was scornful of the Spaniard's flight. Martell defended him.

'It was wise. He did not expect to see me tonight. I think he'd no idea I was in Rome. He made a quick decision to follow me here and not lose track of me. He was virtually unarmed. He wore his rapier as a gentleman would – a finishing touch to his dress but practically useless in that crippled hand of his. Luckily the only pistol was in *yours*.'

It was their one bit of luck. This was not Frankfurt but Rome, where Gonzalo could count on the full support of the Spanish ambassador and of the papal authorities. Within an hour or two he would have watchers in every gatehouse leading out of Rome, and armed horsemen available to pursue any suspected fugitive.

But even Gonzalo needed that hour or two, especially so early in the day, with so many different gates and roads to cover. Only now could he be starting to get the authorities moving. Martell and Giles had that same brief interval and must make the most of it.

Though the deaf old widow had heard nothing of the incident outside she was an early riser and was now hobbling about. They could settle their reckoning, but told her nothing of their plans. As they hurried along the road Martell said: 'We had better start with a ten mile walk.'

'It's the cool of the day,' said Giles thankfully.

Hiring horses at this early hour would delay them slightly and they were more likely to be remembered by someone. Gatekeepers would notice two early riders more than just another man and boy in the growing stream of pedestrians.

Ten miles or so would bring them to the first posthouse outside the city. If no one had already stumbled on the road they had taken, they would be able to hire horses at this staging post and then proceed at top speed.

There were several possible routes northwards from Rome. Gonzalo would send parties along each of them simultaneously.

'Luckily,' said Martell, 'we shall be on none of them.'

'But – how shall we change horses? Where does *this* road lead?'

'Ancona.'

'Where's Ancona?' The name had never featured in their plans for the grand tour.

'It's a port on the Adriatic coast. A place to sail across to Ragusa – or Greece – or—'

'But we're not going to those places.'

'But we want to get back to Venice. And there's a constant traffic up and down the coast. We shall take passages on one of those craft – if possible making no calls en route. So we shall travel night and day. Time-saving and restful!'

It would be welcome after the hard riding that lay ahead. It was about a hundred and eighty miles to Ancona by the Via Flaminia. Those first ten miles of walking took them nearly three hours, for every time they heard galloping hoofs behind them it seemed wise to step aside into a wood or other form of cover. Martell was taking no chances till they felt safe from pursuit.

He had the chance now to explain what he had discovered that enabled them to turn for home. Why indeed it was their duty to do so.

Giles never heard exactly what had happened to give his companion the vital information he wanted. But in the course of the previous night and evening, before his encounter with Gonzalo, he had learnt something which would shake the Queen out of her indecision.

Over the past weeks he had collected, bit by bit, the details of the way other parts of Europe were being drawn into the grand scheme which King Philip was referring to as 'the enterprise of England'.

Some of these scraps he had passed on to Giles but only now, as they walked, did he paint the full picture that had been forming in his mind – and confirmed last night as true.

The armada itself, the ocean-going fleet that would sail across the Bay of Biscay to the English Channel, would number several hundred vessels, the towering galleons in squadrons of a dozen each or more. Philip had recently seized power in Portugal, and the Portuguese were contributing a separate squadron of a dozen galleons.

'They alone will carry over three thousand troops,' said Martell, 'besides their crews. So – you can imagine.'

There were galleasses from the Spanish kingdom of Naples – one even from the Duke of Florence, with a promise of six hundred armed men. There were galleys with thousands of oarsmen and smaller craft of all kinds.

This fleet, the Spanish ambassador had told the Pope, would sail up the Channel, cutting through any English opposition, pass the Straits of Dover, and make a landing at a point which Philip called Cape Margate. With this base it could cover the crossing of an even larger force of soldiers which would have mustered in the Low Countries. Already hundreds of flat-bottomed boats were being collected there to carry the thousands of pikemen and musketeers, the cavalry and their chargers.

'Everything has been thought of,' Martell went on admiringly. 'The commander of the first landing party at Margate is to be Don Alonso de Leyva – a fine man, he leads the light cavalry of Milan. But he will hand over to the Duke of Parma when the Duke arrives with all his forces from the Continent.' A shadow came over his face. 'God knows what the Queen can muster against them if they once land! They're the most formidable troops in Europe. They *mustn't* land.'

The Pope was determined that they should. He was fired now with this dream that heretic England should be reconquered for the faith and Elizabeth replaced by a Catholic queen, Philip's daughter, the Infanta.

'I heard last night,' said Martell, 'of the promise he's sent to Philip through his ambassador. The day the first Spanish soldier sets foot on English soil he'll donate a million gold ducats to the cause!'

'That should convince Her Majesty!'

Sixtus was now even more eager than the King. Being himself no sailor he could not understand that it was too late in the season for all these elaborate preparations to be completed and the armada to sail. The enterprise of England must wait now until next year.

'I believe,' said Martell, with a smile, 'that a certain number of dishes have been thrown about.'

Even this delay made it no less urgent to reach Walsingham. The government must lose no time in preparing their defences.

Once Martell and Giles reached the first posting house and could hire horses they were able to push on at greater speed. Even then, it would have been folly to make themselves conspicuous. It was not until the third day that they were able to ride into Ancona.

Now that his grand tour was rushing to a close Giles found consolation that at least its dramatic manner had brought him into country he would not otherwise have seen.

The port was encircled by a positive

amphitheatre of steep hills. Eastwards, barely a hundred miles across the Adriatic, was the vast Ottoman Empire of the Turks, though the Venetians still held the narrow fringe of the Dalmatian coast and a chain of scattered islets. Beyond that was a different world, a Moslem world, stretching away to Asia and Africa.

Arcona was the biggest port on this Italian side between Venice and Brindisi. It was full of foreigners, so a couple of English faces were unlikely to be remembered.

Martell wanted the quickest possible passage to Venice, a vessel that would waste no time on leisurely stops along the coast. He was lucky, when he enquired at the harbour, to meet the skipper of a small felucca about to leave for Venice with a full cargo for that city, and no intermediate calls.

'Is the tide right?' asked Giles eagerly.

'There *is* no tide on the Adriatic! He'll cast off as soon as we go aboard.'

The felucca was a graceful craft, with long beaked prow and projecting stern. It had two triangular lateen sails and a few oarsmen for extra speed. It was ideal for their purpose. A light wind but fine weather. Cloudless skies and almost a full moon, so that a captain with a life's experience of this coast could keep moving in the night hours.

'I think we have earned a restful day or two,' said Giles. 'No one can get at us here.'

'I should think not,' Martell agreed. But for once there was to be something that not even Martell had thought of.

Chapter Fifteen

What bliss, Giles thought, many times over those first two days and nights.

No dust forever in one's eyes and nostrils, no sweat if one kept in the shade of the sail curving overhead, no jogging horse beneath one, hour after hour.

Instead, the gentle gliding of the felucca, not much faster (he guessed) than his own walking pace – but so effortless, hour after hour. The freshness of the salty air. And the scenery gliding slowly by, just a few miles away, bold mountains at first, then a flatter landscape, like an endless tapestry silently unrolled.

They had better make the most of it. Once past Venice and on roads again, it would be hard going until they reached England. Martell had not yet decided whether they would ride across France or sail down the Rhine to the sea.

It was a pity they would not pass Padua. But he had prepared himself all along for that.

Anyhow – he told himself firmly – it could not have led anywhere.

On the third morning he woke early. Indeed, it hardly was morning – the light slanting into their little cabin was from the moon. He would not have woken, probably, but for faint sounds stirring overhead.

Not footsteps – Francesco's men were silent on their bare feet. But these tense, urgent murmurs? They did not know what a whisper was. Their normal communication was by full-throated yell.

What was going on? He pulled on his trunk hose. Martell had not stirred. No sense in waking him without good reason. Unused to going barefoot, Giles slipped into his shoes and crept out on to the moonlit deck.

The silver brilliance died abruptly, just as he stepped into it, as though the moon had vanished behind a cloud. Staring up he saw that it was no cloud but the vast dark triangle of the lateen sail, which several phantom figures were hoisting inch by inch under the almost silent direction of their captain.

Old Francesco saw him and turned, his hand raised in warning, as Giles began to speak.

'Keep your voice down, signor! The least sound travels across the water. But I fear we have been seen already . . .'

151

Giles crossed the deck, through the shadow of the sail, to the starboard rail still glittering in the moon.

Eastwards, a mile or so further out, was a two-masted brigantine. It was changing course in their direction. It had oarsmen, like a galley, as well as that spread of sail. Perhaps eight men to each of those long flashing oars. It could manoeuvre independently of the wind.

He was conscious of the captain at his elbow. 'A brigantine,' said Francesco softly. 'The pirates' favourite craft.'

'I thought that since that battle at Lepanto—'

'That was years ago. The Barbary corsairs are getting bolder again. All the time. With luck we shall outrun them.'

This was a desolate stretch of coast, with no port for miles to offer refuge. 'But at least I *know* these waters,' the captain went on reassuringly. 'I can venture closer in – take chances they might not dare to. I shall! I don't mean these scum to get hold of me again. Or any of you.'

Giles had already heard of his grim experiences as a youth. Two years as a Turkish captive, slaving as an oarsman in their galleys. Then, by good luck, ransomed – but at great cost to his family. Giles wondered what would happen to him, and to Martell, if these fiends laid hands on them?

One of the sailors offered cold comfort. 'They'll not harm a good-looking young lad like you! You'd fetch too high a price from some rich pasha – to dance attendance on the luscious girls in his harem. Only *you'd* get little enough pleasure from them.' Panic-stricken himself, the man hinted at the horrors threatening Giles. 'You'd not be let inside the harem till they'd made you harmless.'

This time Giles almost froze. Having spent his childhood in the country he caught the man's meaning. Ever since he could remember, he had known the difference between a bullock and a bull. Better a galley-slave on the rower's bench than lose his manhood.

'That's enough, Giuseppe!' The old captain no longer kept his voice down, for obviously the corsairs were now in hot pursuit. '*You're* not too grand for the rowing bench. Best get busy on ours.'

Their own little craft had provision only for three oars a side, used mainly for handling the felucca in awkward docking situations or when completely becalmed. There was no manpower for more, and no need.

Giuseppe joined his shipmates. The men bent desperately to their oars. There was nothing else they could do until the brigantine overhauled

them and its savage crew had to be fought off
with the cutlass.

Giles stayed at the rail, heart pounding, es-
timating the superior speed of the brigantine.
The sky behind grew pink with dawn. Martell
appeared beside him, fully dressed, rapier belted
on his hip.

'Francesco is running for the shore,' he said.
'It's tricky here – shallows and bumpy little
islands, swampy. At least he knows it better than
our friends yonder. And for all our cargo we
draw less water than they do.'

Giles switched his anxious gaze westwards.
The shore stretched its low line of reeds and
tangled grasses. To his dismay they were not
heading straight for it. At this point, Martell
explained, there was no inlet – if the brigantine
caught up with them they would be at her mercy.
But a mile or two northwards Francesco knew
of a gap through which their smaller vessel could
slip into a spacious lagoon behind.

'If we can't reach that . . .' Martell paused,
'we must give them as hot a welcome as we can.'

His rapier was not the ideal weapon for a
rough and tumble. Giles, in his role of young
manservant, had equipped himself with a short
broad-bladed sword, not so gentlemanly but
perhaps more practical. They had a pistol each.

'I doubt if we'll have time to reload,' said

Martell. 'But even two shots may be useful, at point-blank range.'

They would be desperately outnumbered by the swarm of corsairs whose brown faces were now visible. But Martell said encouragingly, 'We can rule out half – no, more than half – of the men aboard her. They're only oarsmen. You need so many for that number of oars. And they're chained to them.'

'But when they get close alongside—'

'They aren't such fools as to loose them from their chains and expect them to become fighting men. Why should they fight *us*? Most of them are probably Christians. Captured and made slaves. They'd jump at the chance to turn on their masters.'

It was unlikely the corsairs would give them the chance.

The felucca plunged gamely forward, every stitch of canvas strained, the few crewmen at the oars pulling manfully to add a fraction to her speed. But the brigantine was creeping nearly level, though further from the shore.

Old Francesco was yelling something and waving his arms. He seemed to have sighted the gap he was looking for in the tall marsh-grasses. If only they could reach it in time!

A cannon roared. The ball went skimming

across the water. It vanished well ahead of them, sending up a fan of lacy foam.

'Missed!' cried Giles exultantly. 'Bad shot!'

'I fancy they didn't mean to hit us. Just a warning shot across our bows. This isn't a naval battle. They want to catch us, not sink us.'

Yes, that was obvious really. What profit would there be in a cargo at the bottom of the sea? Or in a drowned crew instead of prisoners who would fetch a good price as slaves?

The felucca did not slacken speed. Another cannon went off. This time the ball smashed into the bows. The vessel reeled over to port, straightened up with an obvious effort, then staggered on.

The corsairs were closing in. Giles saw the narrow inlet which might spell deliverance. Only another hundred yards. Had they time – just time – to make it?

A third cannon-shot. A crash, this time right overhead. Giles went sprawling. Before he could stagger to his feet a great weight of sail-cloth descended. He was flat on the deck again, breathless, blinded by the sail spread over him.

Somehow he fought his way back to daylight and fresh air. The felucca no longer sped forward. It merely rocked without purpose. The crew were clustering, cutlass in hand, on such clear patches of deck as were left to them.

The brigantine came alongside. Black-bearded turbaned faces glared down at them, muscles were tensed for the moment of the leap. Giles breathed a prayer. His grip tightened on his sword-hilt.

And now they came hurtling over, like giant black ravens against the sunrise. Blades clashed, Martell's pistol banged, Francesco's men howled back defiance.

A pirate made for Giles, a burly figure, even more monstrous in his billowing white trousers. He was shouting something, presumably an invitation to surrender. He wanted (Giles later guessed) a 'pretty boy' to sell in the slave market, unscarred and undamaged. That scimitar would have knocked Giles's sword from his hand. He pulled the trigger of the pistol in his left hand and at that range he could not miss. There was a gasp, a spurt of blood, the corsair fell backwards and vanished under the men who came surging after him.

One rushed at Giles, eyes glinting at the prospect of an easy prize. Sword and scimitar clashed. Sure enough the curved blade, with the man's strength and experience behind it, sent the shorter weapon clattering to the deck. In a battle, that would have been the end of the matter, certainly the end of Giles. But to the corsair Giles was worth more alive than dead.

He lowered the scimitar and shot out his other hand to grab the boy's collar.

Only it was no strong collar, firmly stitched to a jerkin of the same material. It was a white ruff, light as air. It came away at his snatch, and Giles went staggering sideways, free but unarmed.

There was no time to look round for his sword or pick up one of those strewn across the deck. With nothing but the empty pistol in his pocket he saw only one hope.

That last cannonball had snapped the mast like a dry stick. The lateen sail had fallen. Most of it had reached the deck, where the huge canvas triangle lay in its crumpled folds. Some had fallen only part of the way, and dangled from just below the jagged stump of the mast, along with a jumble of snapped shrouds and other cordage. One expanse of this rigging, squared like the mesh of a huge fishing net, seemed to offer a ladder of temporary escape.

Giles jumped. The rigging swayed backwards as he gripped it and found a foothold. But it held, taut under his weight, and still held as he climbed. The scimitar swept vainly beneath his feet.

Would the man climb after him? Not much sense in that. They could scarcely continue the struggle at the shattered end of the mast, each needing one hand to grasp the rigging. But Giles could not stay on that perch for ever. He looked round him with despairing eyes.

And saw something which none of the men struggling below could yet have seen. A third ship no more than a mile away, one of those splendid slim Venetian galleys, its banks of oars flashing in unison along its almost unbelievable length. It was changing course, curving shorewards.

Someone else now saw it. The lookout man on the brigantine. Urgent voices babbled, passing on the warning. Peering down, Giles saw that the corsairs were detaching themselves from the close-quarter struggle on deck, backing towards the rail, jumping and scrambling aboard their own vessel. Now there was a bright strip of clear water, quickly widening, between the two craft.

He lost no time in his own descent to the deck.

He was relieved to meet Martell face to face. Martell looked equally relieved. He assured Giles that his squirrel-like – or even monkey-like – escape up the rigging had been common sense not cowardice. His own right sleeve was darkly soaked in blood, but he made light of the wound.

Old Francesco himself, unhurt, came up to take stock with them. One of the crew was dead, two wounded. The others were dragging tur-baned bodies across the deck and dropping them over the side. They did not pause to check whether the corsairs were alive or dead.

The brigantine was in flight towards the open sea, the galley in pursuit. The galley would prob-ably not return to their aid. They must look after themselves.

Francesco apologized that he could not keep his promise of a swift passage to Venice. With no mast and few oarsmen the felucca could only limp along the few miles to the next port. He could not guarantee there would be another craft there to which his passengers could transfer. Or how long it would take to get a new mast fitted.

With infinite regret he could only recom-mend them, if their journey was urgent, to take the first opportunity to land and make their own arrangements.

Martell agreed. He surveyed the reed-fringed marshes. 'Land us where you can, wherever there is a road. We are good walkers. We'll follow the coach road until we can hire horses.'

'I am sorry,' said the captain. 'There *is* no coast road.'

'No coast road?'

'You see these marshes? In a few miles we come to a wide lagoon – all water and swamp for a long way inland, with no continuous land for walking along the seaward edge.'

He could however set them ashore where a road led westwards, admittedly the wrong direction for Venice. 'But it would take you to Ferrara, which is less than fifty miles, and from there you could swing off to Padua, and from Padua . . .'

Giles waited with bated breath for Martell's decision.

'I think,' said Martell, 'that would suit us very well.'

Chapter Sixteen

It was odd, but Giles felt more scared even than in that unnerving encounter with the pirates. Probably because there was now more time to think.

Martell was more badly hurt than he admitted. For the first time since Frankfurt Giles knew that the responsibility lay on himself. Martell was tight-lipped and pale. His arm was oozing blood again. Francesco had bound it up as well as he could before they left him. But Martell had lost a lot.

Mercifully they found horses not far along the Ferrara road. Martell scrambled awkwardly into the saddle but, with his sound left hand, controlled his mount normally. He had slipped his purse to Giles. 'You must be paymaster for the moment.' Their time in Italy had by now made Giles familiar with hiring charges and other expenses. If he felt he was being cheated

162

he exchanged glances with Martell. The bill was usually adjusted.

They kept up a reasonable pace. Martell could not have managed more. Giles told himself that there was no need for breakneck haste. They wanted to get to England as soon as possible, they would not be out of the wood until they were out of Italy – but at this moment they could hardly have any pursuers. That dash to Ancona, the felucca, the unpredictable attack by the corsairs – not even Don Gonzalo, with all his informants, could have kept up with their zigzag movements.

Martell had a restless night at Ferrara. As he tossed wakefully in the darkness Giles feared lest he had started a fever.

What would they do then? Find a doctor? He had hoped that they could reach Padua. Padua had the finest doctors in Italy. Martell had met some of them. And with the Niccolinis as friends – they *must* somehow get to Padua.

Giles himself slept uneasily, but, when he woke, was relieved to find Martell now sleeping quietly with no sign of fever. When he opened his eyes he seemed cheerful but was clearly very weak. Giles felt that, even if he could sit on a horse, he could not for a long day under an Italian sun.

The sympathetic innkeeper was impressed

when he learnt that the wound had been received in beating off Barbary pirates. Martell should travel on to Padua in a comfortable coach. That would take two days, but the gentleman was in no state to be rattled over the distance in one.

Martell agreed meekly, which showed Giles in what a poor way he must be. He felt more than ever responsible.

'You are looking after me most splendidly, Giles!'

'You're a very valuable property, sir. I'm sure Sir Francis—'

Martell raised a warning finger to his lips. But the old twinkle was coming back to his eyes.

When they reached Padua he wanted to go to the bookshop rather than the Niccolinis' house. 'We mustn't take their hospitality for granted. We'll say we're going to an inn.'

'I don't think we should do anything of the sort, sir. We'd give mortal offence,' said Giles firmly.

'Very well. After all, you seem to be in charge.'

'I *am* in charge, sir. For the moment.'

By good luck Peppina was the first person they saw as they approached the impressive portico. Her eyes widened; she hurried forward to greet them.

'How fortunate! In another two days I should have missed you!'

'Missed us?'

She flushed. 'I should say, my father would have missed you. He is going to Venice. I am going with him.' She tried to sound casual. Then she changed the subject hurriedly. 'But, *Dottor* Martell – what have you done to your arm?'

'It was not what *he* did to it,' said Giles. 'It was a pirate's scimitar.'

'It is nothing,' said Martell.

But Peppina took his undamaged arm in her gentle fingers and drew him, exclaiming sympathetically, along the marble gallery to the room upstairs where her mother was sitting.

What a relief it was to be among such friends again! And to be able, for once, thought Giles, to speak freely about all that had happened in the last few days. The adventure with the corsairs had nothing to do with their secret mission. He need not watch his tongue.

Indeed the pirate incident had transformed them into heroes. When her mother took charge and began to fuss round Martell, Peppina remembered his own existence again, swished round, and bombarded him with excited questions.

All was now bustle. A maid was sent running for one of the city's leading physicians, another to the bookshop to tell Signor Niccolini who had arrived. Clean linen, warm water, and cool wine were assembled with magic speed.

How quickly had the horrors of recent days given place to this happy glow of glory! The eminent doctor arrived and pronounced Martell's wound as not dangerous. No bone shattered, no vital sinew cut. With skilled dressings and ointments recovery would be swift. He would be fit to travel in a couple of days, especially if he went in one of the comfortable barges down the placid Brenta and across the lagoon into Venice.

'They can go with us,' cried Peppina delightedly.

'It would be the best way. No riding, no bumping in a coach.'

The doctor refused a fee. It was an honour to attend the learned and distinguished Englishman.

So all was arranged. How convenient, thought Giles. He could have hugged himself. There was only one shadow on his own luck: the reason for the Niccolinis' visit to Venice was to discuss Peppina's future marriage to the son of her father's friend.

As a hopeless heretic, he told himself, he would not let it cloud his day. It was a day he meant to enjoy. He would look back on it as the climax of his grand tour.

The Brenta barge was the perfect way to make the journey between Padua and Venice. That was why Martell had avoided it when they first came – it was the obvious route any investigator would check after that suspicious episode at the Arsenal. Now, with that behind them, they could safely travel in the reverse direction.

And very pleasant it was. The Brenta, born as a little Alpine river, had been tamed in this final stretch to a quiet, straight, emerald waterway, with a towpath for the horses which pulled the barge. This was a flat-bottomed comfortable craft with a canopy arching overhead to provide shade. It carried passengers and goods regularly between Padua and Venice. Pietro Morelli, the barge-master, was an old family friend of the Niccolinis. Peppina was clearly a special favourite of his. He knew the reason for her journey and meant her to enjoy this memorable day.

On both sides the country stretched flat and fertile, with well-tended gardens and groves of orange and fig. At intervals there were elegant villas, much favoured by the well-to-do Venetians. Many had been designed by her Uncle Andrea. To own a 'Palladian' villa was the fashionable dream.

Only once in the first hour was the calm of this quiet scenery broken. A thunder of hoofs was heard behind them. Four horsemen shot past in single file, startling the two patient beasts towing the barge. The boatman leading them raised his fist and shook it at the disappearing cavaliers.

'Spaniards, by the look of them,' said Peppina's mother in disgust. Giles was learning how unpopular Spaniards were with many Italians. They held so much of Italy. They held so much of the world.

'I just hope,' went on the signora, 'they are not rushing to board our boat at the next stopping-place.'

But they proved to be, and Giles was more dismayed than she was. One horseman, the postboy, was gathering all the horses, to take them back to their stable. The other three men were filing aboard the barge.

The one in front, Giles now saw, was Don Gonzalo.

Chapter Seventeen

Giles felt as if his heart had stopped. What was to be done?

These Spaniards could not lift a finger against them on the barge. The crew would stop them. So would other gentlemen on board. But once he and Martell stepped ashore in Venice how would they shake off these shadows? What other forces could Gonzalo call upon?

Could they, Giles wondered, make a dash for it at the next landing-place? At the very last moment, as the barge moved on again, jump off and run?

Hopeless! The Spaniards would simply leap after them. Once away from the river the fugitives could count on no help.

Giles instinctively shrank into the background, moving a few paces aft. But Gonzalo had seen him and, having paid their fares to the barge-master, was looking for a patch of shade. He paused by Giles, his one gloved hand laid casually on the rail, and murmured softly, 'So I was right. An Englishman – and a youth. Well worth that sweaty gallop in the morning heat! What better company on the way to Venice?'

'If we go that far,' said Giles. Admit nothing. Keep him guessing.

'In such company I will gladly travel any distance.'

'You'll find us poor company. Little to talk about.'

'Signor Martell may talk more freely than you imagine. We may meet friends of mine who will encourage conversation.' There was a sinister tone in Gonzalo's voice. 'You too may help.'

'*I* may?'

'His concern – for your welfare – may loosen his tongue.'

Giles guessed his meaning. The Spaniard would stick to them until, as was sure to happen, he could get help and have them arrested. They would be interrogated. Giles shuddered. He had too vivid an imagination. Martell, he felt sure, could hold out against a great deal. But in his unsentimental way Martell seemed genuinely fond of him. If he had to watch Giles put to torture – an innocent boy he had landed in this trouble – what would he do?

He must speak to him. Giles felt he could not go back and resume his light-hearted chat

170

with Peppina. He must discuss things with Martell. They could talk freely in English. Neither enemies nor friends would understand.

Martell, not surprisingly, was looking thoughtful. 'This is a little awkward,' he said.

'I should say so.'

'But not hopeless.'

Giles could only pray that he was right. 'What can we do? In Venice we'll be at his mercy.'

'Not entirely. Thank God it *is* Venice. And he's Spanish.'

'But they're allies.'

'Reluctant, though, the Venetians. And proud of their independence. They won't let anyone walk over them. Not Rome, or Milan – or Philip of Spain himself.'

Venice, thanks to her special position on the lagoon, had never been occupied by a foreign enemy. But she was contributing those galleys to the armada.

'And they're strict about regulations,' said Martell.

'I remember, sir – when we first came. The fuss there was, checking our documents, to make sure we hadn't been anywhere with the plague! At least there should be none of that today.'

But regulations, Martell pointed out, were not only about health and quarantine. If

Gonzalo denounced them to the authorities as English spies, the case would be taken out of his hands and they would be subjected to patient law-abiding investigation in a Venetian jail. 'That wouldn't suit him at all. He wants a free hand with us!'

Giles could imagine that only too well.

'But it won't suit us either,' Martell pointed out. 'There'd be delay. And we must get to England quickly.'

'What can we *do*?'

'I fancy Gonzalo will let us walk ashore, follow us and watch for his chance to strike. Whichever road we take, he won't lose track of us again.'

'Then it's hopeless.'

'No.' Martell's brow was knitted with concentration. 'If we had a day's start – a few hours even . . . But we can't leave Venice till I've drawn some money on my letter of credit. We'll need the fastest horses we can hire, we may need to give a bribe now and then – we must not be short of funds. And while we go to the banker . . .'

Gonzalo, depend on it, would be mustering a band of cut-throats to stop them on the road. Such men were as easy to hire as horses.

'How *can* we shake him off now?'

'I have just had a wild idea. It may not work. Something you said.'

172

'*I* said?'

Martell would not explain. He had a look of intense concentration. Giles racked his brain to recall anything useful he could have said. But he knew it was useless at such moments to cross-examine his tutor. Martell walked away, avoiding further discussion.

For some minutes Giles stayed unhappily where he was. It would be hard to conceal his state of mind from the Niccolinis, but how could he confide in them without explaining the whole situation – and betraying Martell's secret? He could not avoid them for ever, though. He must go back, and do his best to seem unconcerned.

There was, however, a new difficulty. He had lost his seat between Peppina and her mother. It had been taken by, of all people, Martell. He no longer had the tight-lipped concentrated look of a few minutes before. He was chatting to the signora with an ease that Giles could only envy.

'I understand your daughter – rather unusual for a young lady – has a most scholarly command of Latin?'

'So they tell me, *dottore*. I do not understand a word, myself.'

'Would you permit me to test her?'

'Why not? I'm sure Peppina would be flattered.'

Giles retired, unnoticed and disgruntled. He had never thought of feeling jealousy against Martell. He was soon relieved, though, for the Latin test, and the whole conversation, did not take long. Within a few moments he spotted the girl further along the deck, deep in conversation with the old barge-master. Knowing that she had been Pietro Morelli's pet almost since babyhood, he did not intrude upon them.

He transferred his gaze to Don Gonzalo's companions. They had casually drifted up to positions near the gangplank. The barge was approaching the next stopping-place. They must be holding themselves ready in case their quarry made a sudden dash ashore.

But when the crewman pushed out the plank no one made any sudden dash. Only the barge-master, with an apology to Peppina, broke off their conversation and stepped briskly on to the towpath. He had much to superintend in these brief halts – goods to land and load, fares to collect, friendly greetings to exchange. Eventually he clambered aboard again, the cable tightened as the great draught-horses jingled forward, and the barge began to glide through the green water.

To Giles's relief Peppina finished her conversation with the briefest word, turned, and came briskly and bright-eyed towards him.

174

'I trust you enjoyed your Latin test?' he said.

That seemed to startle her. 'You heard us?'

'I didn't listen. I don't eavesdrop. So I didn't stay.'

She looked relieved. She very gently squeezed his arm as they moved back to the seats beside her mother. 'What an interesting man he is,' she said. 'I had never realized . . .'

They resumed their places and he tried to resume their former conversation. It was hard though to show proper interest in yet another superb villa Palladio had once built on the grassy bank sliding past them. His admiring comments must sound mechanical, his questions automatic. His mind ranged ahead. What would the next few hours bring?

It was reckoned twenty-five miles to Venice, the last five across the open lagoon. On horseback the first twenty could have been covered at speed, but few travellers wanted speed on the delectable Brenta canal. For the whole trip the barge allowed the best part of a day. How would he get through the time?

His suspense seemed in some odd way to have affected the girl beside him. She too seemed to have lost much of her usual spontaneous liveliness. Her questions and answers were becoming as stilted as his own. He must be boring her with his preoccupied responses.

What *was* going to happen? Really, Martell should give him some idea. Had he worked out an emergency plan? He had admitted having some plan forming in his mind, suggested by whatever it was that Giles had said. Martell overdid the secrecy. They were in this together. He owed it to Giles . . .

When he could bear it no longer Giles made an excuse and slipped away, found Martell and demanded in a fierce undertone what to expect.

Martell raised a warning finger. 'Of course. You are quite right, Giles. Listen. In another hour we shall reach Fusina where the barge is hauled over the rollers into the lagoon. That will be the last stop before Venice. If there are no fresh developments by then we'll talk as we cross the lagoon.'

With that Giles had to be content. At least it would put a limit to this nerve-racking suspense.

He rejoined Peppina. Whatever happened in the next hour or two it was sadly unlikely that they would ever meet again. She was to be married next year. This visit was to improve her slight acquaintance with her future husband and his family. If she liked him – and her parents would never force her into a match against her will – the formal arrangements would go ahead.

'If *he* likes *me*, and *his* parents approve,' she said.

'I can't imagine otherwise,' he said in a warm tone, but feeling cold inside.

They were nearing Fusina. The Brenta had given up any pretence of being a natural river. A solid dam blocked the way into the lagoon. Its fresh water must not be contaminated by the brine of the sea outside or the city refuse. Well-to-do Venetians imported pure Brenta water by the barge-load rather than draw from the doubtful wells on their little islands. If any surplus Brenta water went unsold it was diverted into channels to irrigate the fields.

The passengers would have to disembark at Fusina and the heavy cargo be unloaded while the empty barge was hauled over the dam and launched into the lagoon beyond.

'They have an interesting device of machines and pulleys,' Signor Niccolini explained. 'Turned by two horses – like those that work the oil-mills. The barges have wheels slipped under them – there's a wooden flooring so that they can run smoothly.'

It took a little time. There was an inn where travellers could get a drink. Anyone in a hurry need not wait for his barge. There were gondolas for hire, so one could make straight for the city across the glassy expanse of water.

Gonzalo would be well prepared for that. Martell must have realized the folly of making a dash for it at this point of the journey. What *did* he plan? Giles felt for his pistol. Eased his sword in its scabbard yet again. But could not see how either weapon was going to be used in their present situation. How much could Martell do, himself, with that still-unhealed wound in his sword-arm?

The barge drew in to the landing-place. People streamed ashore. The three Spaniards were among the first. Alert for any desperate move by the Englishmen.

Walking behind her parents, just in front of Giles, Peppina let out a little gasping cry: 'Oh, thank God!' Twenty paces away was a little cluster of armed men with an official look. Their leader accosted Gonzalo with a respectful salute.

This was too much. For Giles the bottom had dropped out of his world. Gonzalo was expected. He must have managed to send word ahead of him as soon as he knew he was on their trail. A horseman could have reached Venice hours ago.

But why was Peppina thanking God at the sight of those men? And Gonzalo, apparently, protesting indignantly? And being led away, and the Venetians closing in upon the other two Spaniards?

He caught Martell's whisper to Peppina: 'Good girl!' And, in a louder tone, the cheerful invitation to her parents: 'I think this calls for a glass of wine before we move on?'

Chapter Eighteen

Good manners held Giles back at the hostelry door while his elders crowded in ahead of him. He caught a snatch of the argument as the protesting Gonzalo was ushered across to a boat waiting on the lagoon side of the dam.

'There must be a mistake! We have not passed through any district with plague—'

'Some of the other passengers overheard your conversation—'

'I warn you – the viceroy in Milan—'

'The matter must be investigated,' said the official politely, 'when we reach Malamocco.'

Giles heard no more except a howl of fury as the boat pushed off towards the chain of smaller islands that flanked the city itself.

A radiant Peppina turned to him. Her voice was lowered but her expression almost shouted triumph.

'It worked! I've no idea what this is all about – the *dottore* says I must say nothing, know nothing. I just said what he asked me to say – and Signor Morelli would never doubt my word.'

'You pretended you'd heard those Spaniards say they'd come through an infected area?'

'I said what the *dottore* asked me to say. And to tell no one but Signor Morelli. Not even my parents.'

Everyone in the little hostelry was talking about the arrest of the Spaniards. No one had overheard any talk of plague, let alone reported it to the barge-master. But it would serve the Spaniards right if they now had to spend forty days in quarantine on the island of Malamocco. Even if they proved their innocence they would not get away without at least one night there, which would do them no harm.

'Or us,' Martell told Peppina gratefully.

He was calm and confident now but Giles guessed that under his relaxed manner his usual sense of urgency was there. Gonzalo was not the man to be tied long by the strictest regulations. A key figure in the Spanish security organization, he must have influential links with his opposite numbers in Venice. Once he could get word to them they would soon have him out of the detention centre on Malamocco. The fugitives had best be out of Venice tonight and on some north-ward road to the Alps.

So there would be barely another hour with their Paduan friends as the bargemen took to their long sweeps and sent their craft gliding forward for the last few miles to the Grand Canal.

There must be the parting. The Niccolinis must take a gondola to the house of Peppina's future in-laws. Martell would hire another to the banker who would pay out on his letter of credit. After which he and Giles must take the ferry to Mestre on the mainland and put a few miles behind them before they slept.

It was as well that the Niccolinis' Venetian hosts were not meeting them on the quay when they disembarked. As it was Peppina and Giles had to be swift, and discreet, in their farewells.

'You will send a letter when you reach England?' she begged. 'Address it to my father's bookshop.'

'I will.' He grinned. 'I'd better be quick – for the sake of respectability. Before you are married. I hope,' he said seriously, 'you will be very happy.'

'Oh, I shall,' she promised. And he guessed she would.

Martell was calling that he had got the gondola.

'We should say goodbye in your English fashion. Which the learned Erasmus so highly approved of. You remember what he wrote for his Dutch friends?' Peppina as usual was quoting. ' "Go where you will, it is all kisses. You would wish to spend your lives there." Is it still like that?'

He took the hint, and her response was warm, full on the lips. Erasmus himself would have approved. There was a roar of laughter from the gondoliers standing by their boats. And a scandalized cry from Signora Niccolini.

'*Peppina*! Never let me see you do that again!'

'There'll be no occasion,' said the girl regretfully.

And so they parted.

The day moved quickly to its end. Within a few hours Martell and Giles were riding hard for the north, making the most of the sunset glow.

Within a few weeks Peppina was opening a letter with the news of their safe arrival. And at Taberdars the family were still goggling as Giles regaled them with some, but by no means all, of his experiences. 'It must have been quite an education,' even his mother conceded. 'You might say so,' he answered meekly.

'Well, *that* little adventure is over,' said his father.

Maybe, thought Giles. But not the great one

in which he and Martell had been involved. And in the months that followed he had the feeling that their efforts had not been wasted. Preparations were under way, even in England.

Just as the Queen could not afford to keep up a proper royal navy, still less could she maintain a permanent army like the thousands of soldiers at King Philip's disposal, regular troops, the best trained and equipped in Europe. If the invasion took place, every able-bodied Englishman would have to turn out and enrol in his local company.

Giles would serve with his father and the other gentlemen of the neighbourhood.

'Surely he's too *young*,' his mother protested.

'Plenty of lads no older,' said his father gruffly.

Giles thought of certain incidents on his tour, but he was still bound in secrecy to Martell and did not allude to them.

Spring came, but no Spaniards. It was rumoured that an armada was now really mustering in the Spanish ports, but the weather and other causes delayed their sailing. Then, late in July, at last the Spaniards came.

Olivia had joined her brother for an evening canter on the Downs. 'Look!' she cried suddenly. 'That light!' It twinkled from miles along the coast, a pinpoint against the now darkening west.

'There's another! See! It's the beacons! They're lighting the beacons!'

'Oh, Giles, we ought to go back!'

They wheeled their mounts round and thundered down the well-known track for home.

The Spaniards had been sighted near Plymouth. For the next day or two came constant rumours of their progress. Drake and the other captains had been expected to bar their way, but the winds had given the invaders a chance to slip by. Now they were past Portland Bill, by now they must be off the Isle of Wight – and the English vessels were having to follow, hanging on their flanks.

Here in Sussex many people were afraid the Spaniards would seize the Isle of Wight. It could never defend itself against their overwhelming forces. The Spaniards would make a base there and the whole south coast would be at their mercy, Dorset, Hampshire, Sussex too.

Giles thought these people were mistaken, but they would have ignored the arguments of a mere boy. Once again he could not reveal his inside knowledge or how he had obtained it – that the armada was to stop for nothing till it was through the Straits of Dover and could cover the Duke of Parma's crossing from the Netherlands.

There was a brisk sea-battle off the Isle of Wight but the Spaniards sailed majestically on towards Calais. So Sussex – for the moment – was safe. The Sussex companies were bidden to march to Tilbury at the mouth of the Thames, where there was to be a great concentration of troops to defend London. This, Giles noted, was the right counter-move to the Spanish plan of which Martell had heard in Rome.

Martell's was one of the few familiar faces he saw at Tilbury. His father seemed surprised to see an academic figure like the tutor in such a martial setting – but favourably impressed, and even more so when he heard that he had come down with Sir Francis Walsingham. It was Giles however, not himself, that Sir Francis said he wished to meet.

'You will excuse us, sir?' said Martell politely. 'Sir Francis is naturally much occupied on such a day. But he is free at this moment, while Her Majesty is with her ladies, robing for the parade.'

The Queen had come down by river from Greenwich and was to review her troops on horseback. Sir Francis was in attendance as secretary to her Privy Council.

Giles studied him with interest as he straightened up from his respectful bow. He was a dark, trimly-bearded man in his late fifties, dark-clad save for his decorative ruff – 'Dark as his own doings,' Martell joked afterwards. Giles had so often wondered about him, a human spider at the centre of a web of agents. In the flesh he looked serious but not sinister.

'I have heard much about you, lad,' he said. 'Your tutor gives me an excellent account of you.' He smiled. 'I gather that you learnt a good deal on your travels.'

'I did my best, sir.'

It was the briefest of conversations. But Sir Francis gave the impression that he too could learn a good deal very quickly of anything he wanted to know. 'Our country has need of young men like you,' he concluded. 'I shall hope to meet you again. I must go now to attend Her Majesty. Mr Martell will show you where to stand so that you can hear her speech.' Giles bowed low. When he raised his eyes Walsingham had gone.

Soon he saw the Queen riding through the ranks on a white cavalry charger. She had dressed deliberately in a blend of feminine elegance and warlike splendour. A cloth-of-gold dress and an underskirt of white satin and an imposing ruff, with a polished steel breastplate damascened with gold. She held a marshal's staff and a gentleman-in-waiting carried her helmet with its white ostrich plumes.

She reined in her horse, looked round at the sea of faces, and began to speak. 'My loving people . . .' Giles was never to forget her words. Nor, he was to think in later years, was anyone else. 'I know I have the body of a weak and feeble woman, but I have the heart and stomach of a king, and of a king of England too . . . I myself will take up arms, I myself will be your general . . .'

How she gripped them, that multitude of untrained, ill-armed subjects! Yet she could not possibly know how things would turn out in the week ahead. No one could, not even Martell, not even the well-informed Walsingham. Sixtus, far away in Rome, would be even later in hearing of the fire-ships, and the other events that brought King Philip's dream to disaster. Then Sixtus might smash plates, but he would never have to pay out a single one of those gold ducats he had guaranteed.